BOB KELLY

CHICAGO DETECTIVE
JACK FALLON
IN THE MYSTERY OF THE
EGG OF CHAOS

Dedication

Dedicated to my son Morgan who left this earth way too early
after a long terrible struggle with the scourge of our time

Acknowledgment

Thanks to Morgan Beldock for technical support.

Thanks to Jenna Moudy for her artistic and fashion expertise.

Table of Contents

Chapter 1

The refreshing cool water of Lake Michigan splashed us in the face as it crashed over the bow of the 30-foot fiberglass powerboat we were riding in a few hundred yards offshore of Chicago's North Side. We were heading north on our way back to the Montrose Harbor after enjoying my birthday brunch, having hooked up with some other boaters at the well-known party spot off Ohio Street beach the locals call the playpen.

It was Saturday early afternoon of June 21 on the nearly perfect summer day at 77 with a light breeze from the southwest and mostly sunny skies. My sister Molly brought an array of baked goods from a place called the Coffee Lab which is located near her apartment a few blocks from the Northwestern University campus where she works as a history professor. Our delicious meal included banana bread scones and Mexican curry beef doughnuts and an assortment of iced coffees. My buddy and fellow detective, Ricky Del Signore brought a cooler full of beer and pop and Morgan Latner another good friend and fellow detective captained the boat that he shared with his older brother Reggie and his parents. They conveniently kept it at a slip at Montrose Harbor only a short distance from my apartment in uptown.

Morgan had decided to really open up the throttle and show us just what his 300 hp Yamaha twin engines could do. The sleek sailfish boat powered over the water and through the slightly rippled surface of the lake. After a balls-out ride of a little over a mile, Capt. Morgan let up on the throttle and we cruised comfortably the rest of the way. We rode past Wrigley Field where the Cubs were just getting underway. They were about to play the dreaded St. Louis Cardinals and I could imagine the sights and sounds of the crowd as we passed by. Soon we were in the vicinity of Uptown and pulled into the harbor area and then into slip 66. We got the boat in its slot and tied it off and unloaded our things onto the dock. We said our goodbyes right there since we had parked in several different places with Molly and me having driven separately and Morgan and Ricky having come together from the Edgewater neighborhood. I thanked everybody for providing me with such a nice way to start my 30th birthday.

As I walked through the parking area and approached my black-on-black V6 Camaro a white SUV pulled into a parking spot next to me and a middle-aged guy got out and said, "Excuse me sir. Can I ask you a question?" I glanced back at him noticing what appeared to be a wife and a couple of teenagers in the SUV and replied "sure."

He explained that he and his family were driving across the country for their first time on the mainland. They were from Hawaii. He said they were a little lost and didn't have a GPS system. He pointed out toward the Lake and asked, "Is this the Atlantic Ocean?" I couldn't help laughing a little bit and answered, "No you are about 800 miles short. This is Lake Michigan." He thanked me and got back into his SUV and drove away. I couldn't help thinking how weird that was but if a guy from Hawaii thinks it looks like an ocean that's good enough for me.

On my short drive back to my apartment on N. Clarendon Street, I looked forward to what I hoped would be a relaxing afternoon before going to an art exhibit on Oak Street in the Gold Coast neighborhood. I had been invited to the art show by an attractive young woman named Emma Merlin who was presenting some of her artwork. She was a mesmerizing and somewhat mysterious beauty that I had met at the Green Mill and had been trying only mildly successfully to get to know better. Honestly, I was hoping that this might be a good time to make some progress.

My partner Elaina Rodriguez and I were scheduled to have the weekend off, but we were on call that day between 3 PM and 11 PM, so I knew anything could happen. Days off are always tenuous for a detective.

I got back to my 12th floor apartment at almost 2:30 PM and I sat down on my couch and looked out of my bank of windows facing Lincoln Park and Lake Michigan in the vicinity of Montrose Beach and Harbor where I had just been. I put on some music and laid-back checking some texts and other social media messages wishing me a happy birthday and some other pleasant experiences. I took some calls from several friends and family members as well as my partner Elaina who wished me well and also wished that she didn't see me until Monday. I laughed and thanked her for the positive thoughts.

The rest of the day seemed to fly by. I watched the end of the Cubs game which resulted in a victory over the Cardinals. I counted that as a good omen. I made myself a ham and cheddar sandwich which I enjoyed with some barbecued potato chips and a root beer. I had a couple of Miller's earlier on the lake but I was now on call and had to be cool.

By the time I had gone online to do some work on police reports and to take another cruise through my social media sites, it was time to get ready for the Gold Coast art show and Emma Merlin. So, I took a shower, shaved and donned some khaki pants a chocolate brown short-sleeved T-shirt and a tan cotton lightweight blazer with brown comfortable Rockport walking shoes. I decided to bring a more formal shirt and tie with me just in case the call to duty came.

I hit Lakeshore Drive around 7:45 PM, and on the longest day of the year the sun was up, the skies were clear and the parks and beaches were filled with people picnicking, swimming, strolling and enjoying all kinds of activities including volleyball, basketball, softball and sailing on the lake. With the top and the windows down on my Camaro convertible I felt happy to be a young man enjoying summer life in the great City of Chicago.

I exited Lakeshore Drive at North Boulevard, which is at the north and of the Gold Coast and borders the southern beginning of

Lincoln Park. I made my way south to nearby Oak Street and found a place to park on the street a little over 1/2 a block from the building that was the site where I was about to attend my first actual art exhibit.

I took my invitation out of my glove compartment and walked briskly to the address on Oak Street. I walked up some steps leading to the doorway of what seemed to be a residential building and rang the doorbell. The heavy wooden doors were opened by a tall slender young guy dressed in all black. He said, "Welcome may I see your invitation?" His voice was high-pitched but authoritative which clashed somewhat with his body language and soft energy. He looked at my invitation for what I thought was a bit too long and then dismissively waved me into the exhibit which consisted of a series of connected rooms filled with people and artworks. The first room I entered was fairly busy with people leisurely meandering around the room stopping to look at various paintings' sculptures and pottery. Servers were offering wine which I declined and hors d'oeuvres some of which I accepted.

I didn't see Emma right away so I walked around the room noticing some pretty cool paintings of Chicago sites both people and places and some subjects that I had no idea of what they were getting at. There were a few unusual and attractive pottery pieces and a lot of artsy types that I imagined were wealthy Gold Coast locals.

The next room seemed like more of the same until I spotted Emma. My heart stopped. I hadn't seen her in over two months, but the effect she had on me was very familiar. She was stunningly beautiful, dressed in a salmon red waistcoat with a formfitting teal dress and matching red mid-calf heeled boots. She was about 15 feet away talking to a handsome middle-aged couple who were admiring one of her sculptures which looked to be a cross between a unicorn and a candy cane. She didn't notice me so I slowly moved closer and noticed her name on some paintings including one colorful portrait that struck me as a brooding late-night angry

Johnny Depp. Later I found out that I was right; it was her fanciful depiction of Depp from Fear and Loathing in Las Vegas. Very creative I thought.

Eventually, Emma's would-be customers walked away without buying whatever it was and she looked over and saw me. Her smile stopped me in my tracks and she walked straight to me. Suddenly, the only work of art that I could see was the one standing in front of me. For a long moment we just stood there grinning at each other. She reached out and took my hand only partially snapping me out of my trance. We stopped in front of a standalone artwork placed on a small podium in the middle of the room. The circular object was about the size of a hubcap with swirling interlocking teardrops one of white and the other of blood red, with each having a small circle dot of the contrasting color in the middle of the eye drop. The drops were surrounded by a steel 1-inch-wide ribbon. I had seen the designs before but I couldn't place it.

I told Emma that it was really cool and asked what it was. "It really looks familiar." I thought speaking out loud. She said, "It should. It is the Yin Yang symbol. The Chinese sometimes refer to it as the Egg of Chaos. It symbolizes all of the opposite forces in the universe interacting in harmony. You know the forces of dark and light, hard and soft, male and female etc..."

For some reason, my mind stopped at the male and female part.

"I knew I had seen it before." I said.

She nodded and responded, "It is usually shown in white and black, but it can be done in any number of contrasting colors symbolizing the absence and fullness of color."

"How did you make it?" I asked. She said that she used steel fabricating tools to make the separate teardrops and then painted them and soldered them inside the steel rim and attached it to a short steel base

"Good work. How can you ever part with such an amazing piece of art?" I said trying not to laugh.

"It's easy," she said. "They just offer me enough Yen and they can have the whole damn Yang." At that, we both laughed. She was standing so close to me I could sense her warm breath on my face and feel myself getting excited. She put her hand on my waist and inadvertently brushed up against my gun and holster. She didn't withdraw her hand and moved closer.

"Are you working today, Jack? I was hoping that you could join me at the after party tonight at the Lodge around 11."

"I would love to." I replied. "I am on-call until 11, so if things go well......." My voice trailed off as I felt my cell phone vibrate inside my coat pocket. "Oh crap!" I said out loud.

I reached for my phone and she didn't budge which caused my right hand to brush her perfectly shaped voluptuous left breast. She stayed so close I had a hard time deciding whether to kiss her or check my phone. But duty called and I overcame the powerful urge.

"Damn, and on my birthday." I said in exasperation. "I have to take this Emma. If it turns out to be a false alarm, I'll see you at the Lodge. Otherwise, let's not wait so long the next time." I handed her my card and said, "I hope to see you soon."

"Me too." she replied.

"Good luck. I hope you make a lot of yen." I said on my way out.

"Happy birthday Jack Fallon!" She said. And I was out the door.

I called back to dispatch who told me to head over to an address on N. Astor Street for a fire and possible bombing and homicide. As I climbed into my Camaro, I called my partner Elaina Rodriguez and learned that she had already been contacted by dispatch and would be at the scene in around 15 minutes. She was coming from

11

her home in Pilsen and considering the traffic at 8:30 PM on a summer Saturday night. 15 minutes seemed optimistic.

I however, was less than a mile away and arrived at the chaotic smoke-filled scene in less than two minutes with lights and siren clearing my way. A fire truck was already on the scene and another was just arriving. There were around two dozen people milling about the outside of a four-story townhouse on North Astor Street between W. Schiller Street and W. Burton Place. There were also a couple of patrol cars and four uniformed officers out in front doing the best they could to herd onlookers away from the house.

I was the only detective on the scene and immediately had to take charge. I told the first officer I saw to tape off the front of the townhouse and told the others to try to identify the onlookers who had any useful information. The firemen from the second engine poured into the building which was still bellowing white smoke. They were all wearing masks and carrying fire extinguishers and axes. Others were hooking up hoses and preparing to douse the house. As heavy as the smoke was, I was surprised by the absence of any sensation of intense heat. I approached the front door of the vintage Gold Coast townhouse and practically bumped into a Fire Department Lieutenant coming out and starting down the front steps. He was a large imposing man in his mid-30s and seemed to tower over my 6'2" 200-pound frame as he descended the steps. I identified myself and he said that he had been informed that Lieutenant Whitehead was on his way. I asked him what he could tell me. He hesitated for a second and then said, "Well I'm not sure what it is, but I can tell you what it isn't. It's not a fire. We found a couple of canisters that look like smoke bombs. I ordered the firefighters to leave everything as they find it."

I told him that I appreciated that.

Just then a woman firefighter hurried out of the front door and motioned for us to come with her up the stairs. She said, "Lieutenant you're going to want to see what we found on the second floor." She then made eye contact with me and said, "you too detective."

"The Lieutenant handed me a COVID mask and said, "You won't need a gas mask. It is simply smoky but not toxic." We followed the firefighter into the house and up a wide spiral staircase. I noticed what seemed to be the remnants of a fairly large social gathering of some kind. At first glance, the home seemed to be filled with expensive artwork, rugs and fixtures including a five layered chandelier filled with colored crystals and glittering jewels of gold, green and red hues hanging over a long formal dining room table that looked like it had been partially cleared.

At the top of the stairs, we were directed to the right and into a large old-fashioned study with walls filled with shelves of books and antiques. The room included a large fireplace and a stately mahogany desk and several comfortable looking easy chairs and a leather couch. Behind the desk was a dark leather executive chair which was inhabited by an older well-dressed Asian man. The man was sitting back in the chair with a bullet hole situated between his eyes. Before I had a chance to process the scene, I could hear the sound of footsteps on the fire escape running along the side of the townhouse. The sounds came from above and to my right. I immediately moved toward the door leading to the fire escape landing. Just as I reached for the door, I saw a shadowy figure drop onto the landing and continued down the winding stairs. I quickly unlocked the door which opened directly to the landing. I began barking orders at the firefighters not to touch anything before I bolted out onto the landing of the fire escape and into the smoky dusk.

I missed the first step leading down and swung around almost going headfirst over the railing. I looked down at the concrete tiny patio leading to a gangway between the side-by-side townhouses. I regained my balance and bounded down the stairs. I could see the figure of a small to medium-sized person, dressed all in black including a hoodie pulled tight over his or her head. The figure was

13

well ahead of me but overshot the first-floor landing, and went down a few steps before bouncing back up and entering a small yard and patio set up surrounded by a black wrought iron fence. The figure didn't hesitate and ran toward the fence stepping up onto a patio chair and leaping toward the iron barrier. The acrobat of a person managed to grab onto one of the ornate blunted spikes on the top of the fence and swing himself over in one smooth move. It was astonishing and there was no way I was going to try to duplicate that.

I spotted the gate and hustled through it and found myself looking southward down an alley that was wider and cleaner than most alleys I have ever seen in Chicago. Still, it was getting dark and with smoke still heavy in the warm air, the visibility was not good. I was sure that he ran south but I had lost sight of him. The alley consisted of some small garages and parking spaces, nestled up to backyards and fences along with an assortment of mini dumpsters. I didn't know who I was chasing or exactly why at that moment, but I felt certain that I needed to catch this guy and find out. He was athletic and agile but I was pretty sure he wouldn't have reached more than half a block leading to the next street south. I was somewhat surprised not to see any uniformed officers and quickly called for backup in the alley but I didn't have time to wait. I drew my Beretta 9 mm and moved carefully down the alley zigzagging from side to side. I checked a couple of garages but they were locked and seemed undisturbed. I checked in and around and under some cars and one small blue dumpster but saw nothing. I kept zigzagging across the alley toward another dumpster and crouched low and eased myself around the corner of it.

All of a sudden wham! I was hit with a hard kick to the left side of my face. It staggered me but I stayed on my feet. I recovered in time to block the next kick coming toward my head and grabbed the guy's leg. I twisted the leg as hard as I could and in so doing, I ended up with a shoe in my hand and he landed on his back after bouncing off the dumpster. Just then I felt my right knee buckled and a second kick in my back knocked me down face first. My gun popped out of my hand when I hit the pavement and I got to my knees before taking another kick to the back of my head. This time I was down again and dazed. I was conscious but woozy. I heard a commotion and running footsteps. Then I heard a gunshot and recoiled expecting that I must've been shot. I heard more footsteps running away from me and then the sweet sound of my partner's voice. "Stop or I'll shoot, this is the Chicago Police stop right there!"

I scrambled to my feet and picked up my Beretta and turned to see Detective Elaina Rodriguez. She called in for patrol to look for two slender, short to medium height suspects dressed in black. She looked at me quizzically and asked, "Are you okay Jack?"

I nodded. "We have to stop meeting like this. It's bad for my morale."

She laughed and said, "If I had been a little later, it would have been bad for something else."

We both laughed and I told her, "Thanks partner. You saved my ass again." I couldn't help thinking that this was just the beginning of a very long night and not in the way I had been hoping for.

Chapter 2

Patrol cars started arriving in the alley and we sent two out to look for the assailants dressed in black. I told several other officers to stay there and secure the back of the townhouse.

I then quickly brought Elaina up to speed on what I had seen inside and called in for the Crime Scene Team and reported the apparent homicide. I said that we needed to get back inside the house. Elaina nodded and followed me through the iron gate and up some steps into a back door leading to a large living room, which had been used as a reception area for whatever function had been held there that evening.

There would be time to examine this area later. We needed to get back upstairs to the study. I rushed up the spiral staircase and Elaina followed right behind me. When we got to the study, Fire Department Lieutenant Waskerwitz was walking out. He stopped in the doorway and gave me *the hell happened to you* look. I said, "I know. It's a long story." The Lieutenant waved me inside and said, "Okay save it for your boss." I realized that I looked pretty roughed up. The left side of my face was throbbing and I felt it with my left hand; it was tender and swollen. My hands were scraped and tingling and my pants were ripped on both knees which were surprisingly only lightly skinned.

Inside the study, the smoke had largely cleared and I could plainly see the older man sitting deceased in the executive chair behind the desk. There were a couple of uniformed officers on either side of the desk and in the middle of the room stood the intimidating figure of our direct superior, Lieutenant Tyrone Whitehead. At 6'6" and 240 pounds, the 40-year-old homicide detective was an impressive leader who we had gotten to know during our work on the escort murder case. In fact, he was the reason Elaina and I were recently assigned to his Near North Homicide Unit.

Whitehead had his back to us and when he turned to look at us, I noticed a small slender woman sitting in the chair in the corner of the study to my left that he had been talking to. He greeted Detective Rodriguez and looked me over with another what happened to you look. I gave him a quick rundown and he said that was enough for now.

Whitehead told me to put the rest of it in my report.

He then turned to the lady sitting in the chair and introduced her as Belinda Chin Carlisle Curator of Asian Art at the Art Institute of Chicago. She seemed visibly upset and could barely muster up enough energy to acknowledge us. The Lieutenant explained that she had attended a social gathering there that evening hosted by the Chinese Trade Consulate of Chicago. It had been a cocktail and dinner party attended by a group of guests that either already had or were looking to buy, sell or provide goods and services to entities in China and the United States.

For the occasion it seems that the Consulate had arranged to borrow an extremely rare and valuable artwork from the Art Institute for a private showing at the dinner party. It was a Han Dynasty jade sculpture of the yin-yang symbol created from green and white jade, enclosed in a solid gold band and placed on a small gold platform. It was only the size of a small circular bread plate and not much thicker. It was considered to be well over 2000 years old and a one-of-a-kind. And, it was now missing.

I then understood the shell-shocked look on the Curator's face. But who was the guy with a bullet between his eyes?

Lieut. Whitehead informed us that it was Zhao Chen, the Chinese Consulate General. It had been his party.

Whitehead asked me if I had seen any indication of the ancient artwork. "Whatever it's called." I answered that I had not seen it but that I knew what it was. I said that it was the proverbial Chinese *Egg of Chaos*, the yin-yang symbol of the opposite forces in the universe, balanced in harmony.

Whitehead raised his eyebrows in surprise at my knowledge of the subject. I shrugged my shoulders as if to say *doesn't everybody know that*? I wasn't about to tell them that up until about an hour ago, I had no idea what it was.

"Okay Fallon. He said. "You seem to know something about this thing. I'm going to put you and Rodriguez on the lead for this one. This is going to be complicated, so I want Zilene Baker on it with you."

He saw me wince and followed with, "I know you're not crazy about Kozlowski, but I want Baker on it; so, get over it. You can pick another team. Who do you want?"

I didn't hesitate. "I want Latner and Sanchez.

"Okay you got it. I will see you all in my office tomorrow at 9 AM sharp. In the meantime, finish interviewing Ms. Carlisle and coordinate the canvassing and the crime scene investigation."

Whitehead left the scene and Elaina continued to interview the curator while I looked around a little. I didn't see any signs of a struggle or anything clearly out of place other than the dead guy in the chair. The fireplace was cold and not a book seemed out of place. There were two good-sized dumbwaiters behind the desk that were closed up with mahogany sliding doors. I focused my eyes again on the door to the fire escape.

"Elaina I'm going to check out the fire escape where I saw the guy come down from." I asked one of the uniformed officers to come with me and went out onto the landing, this time much more slowly and carefully. I carefully moved upward in the dark summer night without noticing anything. Soon I was at the top landing looking to enter the fourth floor of the townhouse. The door which was identical to the one in the study opened easily and we entered the dark room. I walked over to the doorway on the other side of the room and flicked a switch on the wall. A ceiling light fixture illuminated a bedroom that seemed untouched. The bed was made perfectly and there were no clothes or anything else laying around. The closet contained some winter coats and boots but nothing suspicious.

I walked out of the room and into a hallway, opened a closed door and walked into a second larger bedroom with a full bathroom and another fireplace. This room seemed lived in by comparison to the first one. The bed was made but loosely. The closets were populated by shirts, pants, suits and shoes. But it was otherwise unremarkable and clean.

Down the hall, there was a laundry room, a full bathroom, and another small bedroom. The bedroom resembled the first one and was quickly cleared. The hallway bathroom was the last room to be cleared and as I opened the door, I saw a young woman dressed like a restaurant server lying on the floor with her right arm and hand resting on the top of the closed toilet. She was cold to the touch and her lips had turned blue. I couldn't see any obvious signs of injury as I called in for an ambulance even though she seemed to be gone.

Then I spotted a syringe on the floor and told the officer to call for someone to get us a NARCAN injector immediately. I started attempting CPR, rubbing her face, arms, and neck; trying to revive her.

Soon there were some firefighters and EMTs on the scene administering NARCAN and trying everything to save her, but it was to no avail. She was deceased. We now had two bodies for the Medical Examiner's Office, a whole townhouse of crime scene evidence and a growing number of mysteries. In a way, it was the detective's dream. And 'holy cow' as Harry Carey would say; Elaina and I were in charge.

I walked back down to the third floor and back to the study. I saw that Elaina was still engaged with Curator Carlisle and pulled her aside to let her know what was going on upstairs, and informed her that I would be checking out the rest of the house.

Down the hall from the study was a large master bedroom with a sitting area, fireplace, full bathroom with a large whirlpool and walk-in shower. The room also had two good-sized walk-in closets. It looked as though someone had been staying there but it was clean and orderly. The CSI guys would give it the close inspection. I wanted to see the whole house. Walking down the spiral staircase, there was still some smoke wafting around, but it was clear that there had been no fire. There were glasses and some assorted plates and silverware still on the large dining room table along with a few ornate candles, one of which was still lit.

On the backside of the main floor which was slightly higher than ground-level, was a large room that had been used to host pre-dinner cocktails. It looked like it was probably originally used as a family room or old-fashioned living room. It had been largely cleaned up but there were still a few glasses and small plates on a couple of coffee tables and there was a portable bar in one corner of the room which had windows on three sides, and which opened up to the backyard patio that I had been in not long before. I looked out and through the dimly lit night I could see the officers and car that I had left there, still in place.

I walked back through the dining room and this time I noticed the dumbwaiters again that I had seen in the study. Since I hadn't seen a kitchen yet I figured the dumbwaiters must originate from a kitchen on the bottom floor. I saw some back stairs leading down. I took them and entered the modern commercial quality kitchen at the lower level. The dumbwaiters were there and one still had some dirty dishes. There were desserts left on the counters and some coffee servers to go with the cakes and bowls of strawberries and cream. There were no signs of a fire as I suspected. There was a door leading out to a gangway and a small table with a couple of chairs sitting at the bottom of the fire escape.

Also on the bottom floor was a large refrigerated storage room in the pantry. There was another laundry room with shelving that held linen towels and cleaning supplies. The dryer was still running and a washing machine was half full of table linen and towels. Everything indicated a rushed exit when the smoke bombs went off. We needed to find out whether any of these people were still around.

I bounded up the back stairs into the dining room, where a couple of uniformed officers were guarding the scene waiting for the CSI people to begin processing the house. I ran up the spiral staircase and found Elaina still talking to Belinda Carlisle. She stopped and pulled me aside and whispered, "Jack this thing is even more complicated than it already looks."

Just then, the technicians from the Medical Examiner's Office showed up to take the bodies. I told them about the second-floor victim upstairs and a few of them headed that way.

Elaina continued, "I don't know who you have upstairs but our victim here is the Consulate General. He's a pretty high-ranking member of the Chinese Communist Party in their diplomatic corps. Ms. Carlisle here says that this was a very high-powered little gathering of some of the business and financial leaders who are either already doing business with China, or who are trying to break into it. I'll have a whole list before I let her go."

"Okay." I said. "I'm going out front to see if any of the guests or Consulate officials are still around."

Outside nightfall had fully settled in on the warm Chicago night, but smoke was still lingering in the humid air. I spotted an elderly man with longish white hair and a white goatee. He was pacing up and down the sidewalk and seemingly talking to himself. I walked over to him and stood in front of him until he walked right into me and jumped back looking startled and alarmed.

I quickly introduced myself and assured him that there was no reason to be afraid. He regained his composure somewhat and asked me what happened. I responded that was I was hoping he could help me with that. "Why don't you start by telling me who you are?"

"Okay sure," he responded. 'My name is Nils Borland."

"Mr. Borland were you inside the townhouse this evening?"

He responded with, "It's Professor Borland. And yes, I was at the dinner party."

"What can you tell me about it?" I asked. He went on to explain that he believes he was invited to the gathering because of his extensive knowledge of ancient Chinese art, and he thinks the Consulate General wanted to impress other guests by showing the rare Han dynasty Jade sculpture of the Egg of Chaos.

He began to explain what it was but I stopped him by saying that I was aware of what it was which definitely surprised him. "You have a knowledge of art history?" He exclaimed.

"Not really." I said. "I just have a little knowledge of what the Egg of Chaos is."

"Tell me about how the evening unfolded."

"Well, I arrived at the party at about 5:30 PM and everyone was there by 6. We were served cocktails until dinner which began at seven. During that time, all the guests were taken in pairs up to the second floor to see this amazing Han dynasty sculpture. It was my whole reason for being there really. I was paired with Belinda Chin Carlisle."

"She had arranged for the piece to be at the party. As our Curator at the Art Institute, she's is the only one of the guests that I know at all. The others are all in business or banking or something. I just wanted to see the Egg of Chaos in person."

"How did that work out for you?" I asked.

"It was magnificent in its simplicity." He responded. "Produced by hand, the precision is incredible and it is in fantastic condition considering it is well over 2000 years old."

"Who was present when you viewed the egg?" I asked.

He answered, "Zhao Chen, the Consulate General was in the study with one of his Deputy Consulate Generals, a young man named Li Yong or something like that and Belinda Carlisle. There was another Consulate Deputy General at the affair named Fong, I think. She mainly stayed with the guests having cocktails."

"Did anything unusual happen during that or at any other time throughout the evening?" I wanted to know.

He explained that the viewing was fairly short and consisted of some small talk about the Egg and Chinese art in general. "The rest of the evening was fine up until the bombs went off of course."

"Where were you when the smoke bombs went off?" I asked him.

"We were just finishing our dinner which was splendid and very pleasant. People were relaxing and dishes were being cleared before we were to be served coffee and dessert. Then bang bang bang suddenly smoke was billowing into the room from seemingly all directions and people started running around in a panic. I hurried out the front door with several others and went into the street. I walked away from the house. The smoke was overpowering and people were coughing; even my eyes had teared up. It was hard to see anything clearly. People kept coming out and spreading onto the street getting into cars and driving away."

"Why did you stick around? "I wondered out loud.

"At first I was just kind of in shock and wasn't in any shape to drive. Then I began to worry about the Egg of Chaos. I knew that Belinda must be freaking out and I thought that I might be able to help in some way."

"Did you hear anything after you came out of the house?" I asked.

"No not really, until I heard sirens and the Fire Department arrived."

I took Prof. Borland's contact information, thanked him and told him I would be in touch.

He asked me what happened and if the artwork was safe. I responded that it was all under investigation and that was all I could tell him.

Just then a full Crime Scene Unit arrived being led by Sargent Gino Barsanti, an officer that I knew and respected. I filled him in on everything I knew and asked him to get in touch with me in the morning.

I kept on interviewing bystanders which turned out to be mainly neighbors who verified that the bombs went off just before 8:30 PM and that there were multiple explosions. Some witnesses said there were two and some as many as five. Also, some reported hearing a popping sound a few minutes after the bombs. Other didn't recollect that. A few of the neighbors that lived in town houses on the block informed me that they had cameras on the outside of their homes and offered to let me see the recordings. One guy, George Townsend lived right across the street. I took his information and assured him that I or someone else would be contacting him soon.

Behind me, I spotted my partner walking out of the townhouse with Curator Carlisle. I approached them just in time to hear Elaina tell the still forlorn lady to take care and try not to worry herself to death. She assured her that we would do everything possible to get her artwork back to the Art Institute. Belinda Carlisle shook Elaina's hand with both of hers and slowly walked away down N. Astor Street and into the warm summer night.

Elaina explained that the crime scene people were swarming the house and think we would just get in their way. She suggested that we continue canvassing the neighborhood including trying to find neighbors in the back across the alley that may have heard or seen something. So, for the next few hours we talked to a couple of dozen more people that we found at home or on the street and took statements from some, and took note of several neighbors in the back that had cameras facing our townhouse and down the alley.

By around 1 AM, the street was very quiet and most of the patrol cars and all of the fire department vehicles were long gone.

Sgt. Barsanti of the Crime Scene Unit came down the front steps and walked over to us. He was holding four evidence bags that each contained a scorched white container. He informed us that these were the smoke bombs they had found so far, and that they would be busy in there all night. He promised to have a report for us sometime later that day. We thanked him and he walked to the evidence van and entered with his canisters.

Elaina looked at me and smiled. "You really do take a good punch." she said with a laugh. I smiled and managed a chuckle before the throbbing in my left temple tempered the humor.

"You know what? I said. "I think it's time to get a beer. I think we've earned It." she agreed and added, "So much for the weekend off. And, it is your birthday after all!"

I gave her a high five and said, "Meet you at O'Toole's." She nodded and I was off on my way to my Camaro down the block. My mind wandered to thoughts of Emma Merlin and her powerful sensuality. I was tempted to head to the Lodge and the after-show party but had to stifle my strong urge. Anyway, I didn't think that it would be a great idea to bring my attractive dark-haired Latina partner and I knew how early my alarm would go off later that same morning. My pursuit of the mysterious young artist would have to wait.

Elaina and I found parking fairly close to Timothy O'Toole's and walked down the stairs and into the busy Saturday bar crowd together. Charlie the cute blonde young woman behind the bar spotted us and waved us toward a couple of open seats in her section. She pulled a Miller for me and a Corona for Elaina put up three shot glasses and filled them with Jack Daniels. We clinked glasses and the shots went down. She filled the glasses again, put the bottle away and said, "Well it seems like we've seen this movie before. Another rough night on the job Jack?"

"Yeah, something like that." I responded. Just then my older brother Barry came up behind us and patted me on the back. He said hello to Elaina and wished me a slightly belated happy birthday. I gave him a general idea of what the evening had been like and asked him how he and the wife and kids were doing. He answered that all was good and promised that we would get together soon for a Cubs game. At that point Charlie came by with a plastic bag full of ice and handed it to me. "Same procedure as last time." she said with a wry smile.

"Looks like this time at least you didn't lead with your chin though." She then went on her way and busied herself delivering drinks to the thirsty throng at the bar.

After a couple more beers, I was feeling relaxed and hardly noticed the throbbing bump on my head. I was ready to go home to recharge my batteries and dive into the challenging case ahead of me. Elaina and I parted ways outside of O'Toole's and I walked to my car feeling once again exhausted and exhilarated to the max

Chapter 3

Sunday morning came a little earlier than usual, at 6:30 after about four hours of deep sleep. I felt surprisingly fresh, wide awake and energized by the bright summer daylight already in full control of the morning. Other than a slight throbbing in my left temple, there was nothing to remind me of the events in the alley behind the townhouse on the previous evening. Except that is, until I went into the bathroom and saw the considerable lump on the left side of my head and a very colorful and impressive black eye.

I took another look at myself, just shrugged and thought, *oh boy, Kozlowski will love this.* I proceeded to shave, shower and get dressed for a summer day on the job. I was excited to dive back into our new case and was looking forward to taking the lead with Elaina for the first time. I kept running what I knew so far about the facts through my mind and thinking about the challenges ahead. It seemed a bit mysterious and somewhat complicated. Little did I know that complicated would turn out to be an understatement.

I placed some English muffins into the toaster and grabbed a bottle of orange juice from the fridge, and winced. The tenderness in my sore right hand was another reminder of my run-in with my unknown attackers in the alley. I couldn't help thinking that I owed somebody some payback.

I sat down in the living room, enjoying the bright view of the park and turned on the TV to see if my case was getting any play on the local news channels. The previous night had not drawn the attention of too much of the local media. After all, it had been a warm-weather Saturday night in Chicago, so there were probably a lot of incidents throughout the city and suburbs.

Flipping through a few news channels, I finally found one that was reporting on the double murder in the Gold Coast. The news anchor was going over some of the known facts and the international implications of the murder of a high-ranking Chinese diplomat. That part of it really got me wondering. I hadn't given the international implications of it much thought. I knew a little about diplomatic immunity and federal jurisdiction issues but had never worked on a case where they came up. I couldn't wait to get started.

Leaving the Covington Apartments at 7:30 AM gave me plenty of time to get to the station on N. Larrabee Street before 8 o'clock. The Sunday morning traffic was light, and I pulled into the station's parking lot around 7:45. Elaina's Jeep was already there as well as several other vehicles.

Inside the detective's room, I greeted Elaina, who was sitting at her desk, engaged at her computer and nodded to Zilene Baker and her partner Frank Kozlowski standing near the coffee table. Zilene smiled and said hi, and Koz started laughing and turned his back to me, mumbling something. We had never gotten along but had recently engaged in a kind of truce. I was hoping that he wouldn't be a pain in the ass, but I was ready to deal with it forcefully if I needed to. This was my case!

Soon my friend and colleague Morgan Latner and his partner Henrique Sanchez came in. We exchanged greetings and a little small talk about what had occurred the day before at N. Astor Street. And then we got the call to report to Lieutenant Tyrone Whitehead.

We all filed into his office, where he had placed enough chairs for all six of us. He motioned for us to sit down and began the meeting. Whitehead went over the general details what had happened in the Gold Coast. He explained that because I had been the first detective on the scene and because I knew something about the priceless artwork that was now missing, he had decided to give me Elaina the lead on the case. He also said that he put Baker and Kozlowski on the team and that I had added Latner and Sanchez.

Whitehead was well aware of my uneasy relationship with Koz, so it was directly aimed at him when he asked whether anyone

28

had a problem following my lead on the case. Everyone nodded and said no problem at all etc., except Koz, who just sat there silently. Whitehead noticed and stood up. He walked around his desk and placed his athletic six-foot-six frame in front of Koz, who now seemed more apprehensive than smug.

"Kozlowski, if you have something to say, I want to hear it now. If you're not fully on board here, I will find Baker a new partner."

Koz sheepishly whispered something that sounded like *okay*. Whitehead was not satisfied. He told him to say out loud that he was completely on board or get the hell out right now.

Kozlowski composed himself and loudly stated what Whitehead wanted to hear. Whitehead nodded, put his powerful right hand on Koz's shoulder and squeezed hard. He then walked back behind the desk and sat down.

"Jack, give us a rundown on what you know about the events on N. Astor Street."

I proceeded to relay everything that I'd witnessed and learned the previous night, including my pursuit of the unknown person down the fire escape and into the alley where he caught me with a sucker punch, kick to the head, and the attack from a second assailant which had been very timely interrupted by the arrival of Elaina which scared them off.

I went over my interviews with the art history professor Nils Borland, and some of the neighbors, such as George Townsend. I described the general layout of the townhouse and the areas where the two victims were found as well as the fact that four smoke bombs were used to cause confusion and the cover to commit the murders and the theft of the ancient Jade Egg of Chaos.

I mentioned the curator Belinda Chin Carlisle from the Art Institute, who had provided the artwork for the private showing, hosted by the Chinese trade consulate of Chicago. I then turned the meeting over to Detective Rodriguez who had interviewed her.

Elaina stood up and picked up right where I had left off. "I was able to do a thorough interview with Belinda Carlisle, who, despite being nearly in a state of shock, was able to give me a pretty good idea of the makeup and basic tenor of the events of last night."

"She explained to me that she didn't know any of the guests at the dinner other than the professor from the University of Chicago Nils Borland, whom she had met several times at various art exhibits hosted by the Art Institute. She had a couple of meetings with staff at the Chinese Consulate, one of which included the Consulate General, Zhao Chen, one of our victims."

Elaina went on to list the guests as Curator Carlisle had recalled them to her. According to her observation, the group seemed to be there more for business purposes than to celebrate the amazing artifact on display.

"The party seemed to be comprised of pairs of competitors that Carlisle found curious. There was a pair of high-tech industrialists, including, Li Zen, the Director of US operations for the Shanghai Power and Technology Company, and current President of the US-China Trade and Economic Forum. He was paired with Grace Tobin, Chief Operating Officer of Future Mindscape Industries, one of Chicago's leading high-tech companies. There were a couple of high-powered financial advisors apparently looking for high-end Chinese clients. Harriet Bingham, the Chief Investment Banker at Chicago First Multinational Bank, was one and the other was a young man named Dominic Blasi, a self-proclaimed financial advisor to the super-wealthy with offices at the Monadnock building on Jackson Boulevard downtown. Two of the largest importers of Chinese products in the US were also represented. Harry Sachman, the Head of Purchasing for America's giant retailer Maxi-Mart was there along with one of his competitors, Francine Vito, the Chief Operating Officer of North American Importers, a major supplier of imported products to competitors of Maxi-Mart with offices in Chicago and New Orleans. Two of Chicago's leading business people from the City's largest Chinese neighborhoods were also present. Herbert Long, a restauranteur and owner of many properties on Argyle Street and the surrounding area in Uptown, was there. His counterpart of sorts was Lily Mai Tong, described by Belinda Carlisle as a strikingly beautiful woman and also a prominent property owner in Chinatown with several business operations, including restaurants and shops in Chicago's oldest Asian neighborhood. The Chinese delegation from the Consulate included Consulate General Zhao Chen and his Deputies, Li Quang Yong, described as a 40 something, tall, slender man, and Fong Wu, a somewhat younger woman with shoulder-length brown hair."

When Elaina paused and seemed to be finished, Lieutenant Whitehead took over again. "Thank you, Detectives Rodriguez and Fallon. Your information gives us a lot to work with for starters." He then motioned for Elaina to sit down and continued, "This case hasn't drawn a lot of media attention yet but it could. I would like to keep it quiet for as long as possible, but I'm afraid that it won't be long before the dam breaks and we get flooded with reporters. This is likely to have national and even international implications. I am surprised that we have not heard from the FBI yet but rest assured we will."

He paused for a second and then continued;

"Detectives Fallon and Rodriguez will take the lead, but I want to be kept in the loop daily at least. There are going to be jurisdictional issues, and the Chinese could be a pain in the ass to deal with. I want full autopsies completed on the victims before either of their bodies are released. Okay, Fallon, this is now your case. I'm counting on you to handle this. Don't disappoint me."

"Yes, sir." I responded and stood up to lead our team back to the detectives' room. Once there, I dove right into organizing our plan of attack. I gave the financial advisors and the high-tech

31

hotshots to Baker and Kozlowski and the big importers and townhouse neighbors, who had given statements, to Latner and Sanchez. Elaina and I would take the Chinese Consulate officials as well as the local Chinese American business guests. We would also immediately go to the Medical Examiner's Office building to ensure that the evidence there was secured.

"Okay, we have our work cut out for us." I said. "We have a great group of detectives here, and I trust all of you to have each other's backs and get the job done. Communication is crucial. So, everybody stay in touch. Let's meet back here at 5 PM today."

Chapter 4

Elaina and I went directly to our assigned Chevy Impala, and my partner prepared to drive as was our usual practice. She was uneasy riding in the passenger seat, and I had grown to enjoy it after doing all the driving with my previous partner Vernon Johnson. He liked being able to keep his eyes on the streets at all times, and I was increasingly finding myself agreeing with him.

During the short drive to the Medical Examiner's building on W. Harrison Street, we had a chance to catch up a little bit about what had been going on the past couple of days. She asked me about how the rest of my birthday went, and I told her about my nice day on the lake with Sister Molly and fellow detectives, Morgan Latner and Ricky Del Signore as well as a brief description of the art exhibit.

I asked Elaina how the repairs on her home in Pilsen were going after the bombing that occurred there in April. She said the renovations inside the house were nearly completed but that the front porch still needed a complete reconstruction. By that time, we had pulled up in front of the large concrete structure, housing the Medical Examiner's Office.

We walked through the security checkpoint and were directed down the hallway to one of the autopsy rooms. Inside we came upon a middle-aged doctor leaning over the table, which held an obviously deceased person. The doctor noticed us and looked up. His dark brown eyes were intense and piercing. We introduced ourselves, and he informed us that he was Dr. Marcello Paez. Neither Elaina nor I were familiar with him. He was short and slightly built, but his deep voice and commanding body language were noticeable.

He was working on the Consulate General Zhao Chen, who seemed to be staring right through me from his prone position on the table. I asked Dr. Paez how the autopsy was going, and he just shook his head and said; *(I imagined him smiling widely through his medical mask before he spoke)* "I haven't gotten too far on this one, detectives. The night shift didn't get to him because of heavier numbers than usual over the weekend. He is my priority today, and I should be finished with him later this afternoon."

Elaina asked him whether anyone else had come by asking about this case. The doctor shook his head again and asked if he should expect others. I spoke up and told him that the Chinese Consulate representatives and Agents from the FBI were likely to drop in. I told him that we wanted the autopsies on the General and the unknown Asian woman brought in last night with him, to be completed before we would give the go-ahead to release either one of them. "Dr., I will be sending some uniformed officers here with orders not to let the two bodies be released to anyone without a Court Order. Do you happen to know where the young woman from last night is being autopsied?"

The doctor nodded and said he thought it was room seven and turned away to go about his business. As we left, he said that he should have a report for us by the next morning.

We found our way to room seven, and inside I spied a familiar face. It was Dr. Lacey Gorman. I was very familiar with her from other cases, and we all exchanged greetings, and she informed us that she was also on her first case of the day with the young woman on the table in front of us. In contrast to Zhao Chen, she didn't appear to have a mark on her. Her eyes were closed, and her face seemed to be in repose. Dr. Gorman was obviously just getting started. I explained the situation to her, including that there would be some officers arriving soon with orders not to release the body without further notice.

She said that she understood and that the final report may take a while since there were no apparent signs of trauma and that it

34

could very well hinge on the toxicology, which might be several days. We thanked her and promised to stay in touch.

When we reached our car, I suggested that we get some breakfast and take a little time to figure out our next move. Elaina agreed, and I said that I knew just the place.

A few minutes later, we pulled into a parking space on E. Erie Street and entered the side door of the enormous building which spans the entire square Block bordering North Lakeshore Dr., East Erie Street, E., Huron Street, and McClurg Court. The bright and comfortable breakfast and lunch place called Eggs Inc. was just up the stairs and to the right. We were seated right away at a table and quickly brought a couple of ice waters. After the friendly young woman took our orders, we had a little time to talk.

I asked my partner what she thought about our mess of a case. "I think we need to nail down some of these moving parts one at a time," she answered. "We need to know whether the two murders are connected, and that will be difficult until we have the autopsy results on our young lady and her identity. We will have to wait on those. We also need to figure out if this whole thing was just a robbery or a murder where the theft was an afterthought. If we can find the Egg of Chaos thing, we should get some answers."

I agreed and added that I thought we needed to learn more about how this little dinner party got put together and who planned it. At that point, breakfast was served. Elaina had a ham and cheese omelet with onions and peppers and wheat toast. I got two eggs over medium bacon home fries and rye toast with strawberry preserves. The coffee refills topped it off and we happily were occupied with an excellent breakfast.

When we were nearly finished, I noticed an attractive blonde woman around my age get up from her table and walk to the counter to pay her bill before exiting. She had a distinctive shortish haircut that was stylishly uneven, which created a sleek modern look. She seemed strangely familiar, but I couldn't place her. Then it hit me.

35

She looked very much like a girl that I had dated briefly in college named Dana. I really liked her and was feeling very good about it and then poof it was over. She didn't answer or return my calls. I kept trying for a while with a few calls and texts, and even a funny card that I was hoping would make her smile, but nothing worked. It has remained a mystery to me ever since.

I heard Elaina's voice, "Earth to Jack. Are you there?" I looked at her and smiled, "yeah, I'm here. Just thought I saw someone that I used to know. Have you ever just lost somebody?" I asked. "Not a family member who died or anything like that. I mean someone you are close to that just disappeared from your life with no explanation. Just proof and gone."

"I don't know. I'm not sure; you mean ghosted?" Elaina started to answer me with a question, but just then my phone started buzzing. It was Lieutenant Whitehead, and he sounded agitated. "Jack, where the hell are you?" He exclaimed.

When I told him where we were, he said, "okay, good, they just got a report of gunshots at the Chinese Consulate only about four blocks away from you. I don't know what the hell is going on, but you and Rodriguez need to get your asses over there, pronto. Keep me informed."

Within two minutes, we were pulling up in front of 1 Erie Street, a six-story glass and steel multi-use building, that houses among other things, the Chinese Trade Consulate of Chicago. Three marked police cars were already there as well as an ambulance. A couple of the first-floor windows were shattered, revealing the inside of a once crowded retail shop. Customers from inside and onlookers filled the sidewalks on both sides of the street as police officers were herding people away from the front of the building.

We hopped out of our Impala and approached the nearest officer. She stopped her crowd control efforts when she saw us approaching. "What do we have here?" I asked the young female officer, who identified herself as Officer Kathy Gibson. She

36

explained that she arrived after the incident, but witnesses reported a drive-by shooting and rapid heavy gunfire coming from a dark-colored SUV. Some of the witnesses thought that the gunfire was directed at some Asian people who were exiting that black Toyota Sienna minivan sitting at the curb right there." She pointed it out for us. I looked to my right and saw the van, which took a couple of dozen shots that blew out most of the windows and created large penetration holes spread the length of the vehicle. Several people were being treated by EMTs and officers for cuts and contusions. Officer Gibson informed us that they were all customers from the retail shop. Miraculously no one seemed to have been directly hit by the gunfire. I directed Gibson to have the other officers who were not needed for crowd control to begin taking statements from any witnesses, but most notably, to protect the crime scene until the CSI people arrived. I asked her if she knew where the passengers from the Toyota van had gone. She motioned toward the front door of the building, which amazingly had remained intact.

As we approach the front door, we could see media trucks from local TV stations arriving on the scene. I looked back at Officer Gibson and grunted, "No interviews with the media." She smiled and replied, "Gladly."

Inside the lobby, a couple of officers were securing the entrance to the shot-up retail shop to the left of the reception desk. Behind the desk sat a pleasant-looking redheaded young woman. Next to her stood a portly middle-aged man wearing a security guard's uniform. When I asked for directions to the Chinese Consulate, she pointed toward the elevators behind her and said, "They have the fifth floor."

I spoke briefly with the officers and instructed them not to let the media or anyone else in. We walked onto a waiting elevator, and Elaina pushed button number five. When the elevator door opened after a quick ride up the fifth floor, we stepped out into a brightly lit hallway and were immediately confronted by three uniformed Chinese military personnel wearing helmets and

37

carrying rifles and sidearms. We were motioned to stop right there, and one of the guards disappeared into the Consulate.

A couple of minutes later, a short slender woman of around 45 years walked out of the Consulate with a huge and powerfully built man dressed in a gray suit with a white shirt and red tie. She had a very calm and professional demeanor. He, on the other hand, had what seemed to be a permanent scowl on his face and was more intimidating than the three-armed guards combined.

We both produced our credentials, and she introduced herself as Hu Ying, the executive assistant to Deputy Consul Gen. Fong Wu. She asked, "How may I help you, detectives?" Elaina responded that we were investigating the incident that had occurred at the party that the Consulate had hosted the previous evening on N. Astor Street, and were of course now interested in the shooting that had just took place outside their building.

Hu Ying said that she understood perfectly that we would want to speak with the Deputy Consul General, but the Consulate was now closed as a safety precaution due to the events we were investigating. She suggested that we check back later in the week. Regular business hours were Monday through Friday, 9 to 4.

I thanked her for her time and handed her a few of my cards, and asked her to give one to each of the Deputy Consulate Generals. "Their cooperation would be greatly appreciated by the Mayor, and the whole City of Chicago." I said with an exaggerated air of self-importance.

Elaina turned away trying to hide her wide grin. Once in the elevator she burst out laughing. "Be sure to say hello to the Mayor for me the next time you two have lunch."

I had to laugh at myself.

"I thought it was a nice touch. Glad you liked it."

Upon leaving the elevator, we braced ourselves to deal with the waiting media outside. Instead, we nearly collided with a man and a woman dressed in gray suits who were standing right in front of the elevator door. I looked angrily at the nearest officer and exclaimed, "What the hell did I tell you!" The officer sheepishly shrugged his shoulders and replied, "I know but you better ask them."

The man stepped toward me and offered his hand. "I'm Henry Chan and this is my partner Teresa Marek, FBI Special Agents." He said as we shook hands. He showed his credentials and said, "We appreciate your officers showing us the courtesy of letting us wait for you here. I hope you have been informed that we would be coming."

"Actually no. I barely got the words out before my phone buzzed. It was Lieutenant Whitehead. He explained that we would be meeting with two FBI Agents who would be joining our team. It had been cleared by the District Commander and the Supervising Agent at the FBI's Chicago office. You are still the lead detective on the case. They should be on the scene soon."

"They are already here Lieutenant." I answered. "As well as a ton of media. Any suggestions?"

"Yeah. Go out the back door."

I turned to the special agents and introduced myself and Elaina." That was our Lieutenant. Welcome to the team."

"Thank you." Agent Marek offered. "We have been asked to follow your lead Detective Fallon. How can we help?"

I was impressed by the professional appearance and collegiality of their approach to the situation. Henry Chan was a wiry man of average height and close-cropped black hair. He seemed to be around 40 years old. Teresa Marek was an attractive woman with medium length, light brown hair, standing about 5 foot four and in her early 30s.

I had the idea that we should head up to the Argyle Street Little Saigon area and scope out the home neighborhood of one of the dinner guests from N. Astor Street, Herbert long. I told Elaina and she said, "Sounds good." I asked the agents if they would like to come along and they enthusiastically answered in the affirmative. I said that I knew a good place called Donang Kitchen at 1019 W. Argyle St. and told them to meet us there.

We went outside and instead of fighting through the now large contingent of reporters and camera operators, I decided to stop and give a brief meaningless statement. Basically, it was that the investigations concerning N. Astor Street and what had just occurred at the Chinese Consulate building were just getting started and there would be more information forthcoming as facts became known.

Elaina and I got into our Impala and the FBI agents got into their Ford sedan and followed us up to Chicago Avenue and then East and onto Lakeshore Drive northbound before we exited at the northern edge of the Uptown neighborhood and the Argyle Street, Asian corridor. We found a couple of metered parking spaces fairly close to the donating kitchen and made our way to the entrance of the traditional storefront Café.

Inside we were greeted by an older but very spry Asian woman, who greeted us with a heavily accented form of English. She ushered us into one of their clean modern tables for four. Menus, waters and a pot of tea were laid out immediately. The atmosphere was simple with white walls and a lower 3-foot border of gray.

The half-full restaurant was accented with some pleasant low decibel music wafting around the room. Besides taking a look at the home territory of one of our dinner guests, I thought that Elaina and I could probably learn some useful insights from our new FBI teammates. It turned out to be a great idea. We learned that Henry Chan grew up in Chicago's Chinatown and now lived nearby in Bridgeport. His great-grandfather arrived in California to work on the railways in the 1860s and his grandparents moved to Chicago around the turn-of-the-century to get away from the extreme anti-

Chinese environment in California at the time. His grandparents opened a laundry and then his parents expanded and added a dry-cleaning operation. He said that his parents and a brother and sister were still running the business in Chinatown. He went to Senn High School and then the University of Illinois in Champaign. He also attended Chicago-Kent School of Law before going straight into the FBI.

Teresa Marek grew up in West Allis, Wisconsin where she attended high school and went on to the University of Wisconsin at Madison. She majored in Chinese Language and went on to get a Masters in Asian Languages and Cultures in Madison.

We ordered a variety of small Vietnamese plates and enjoyed a delicious light lunch. We filled them in on the events at N. Astor Street and the murders of the Consulate General and an unknown young woman. They informed us that they had been monitoring the Chinese Consulate in recent weeks as well as the tongs, the Chinese Street gangs from Chinatown and Argyle Street.

The FBI had noticed a significant uptick in chatter between the On Leong affiliated gangs in Chinatown and the Hop Sing affiliated gangs from Argyle Street. They weren't sure what was going on but they have been concerned that there seems to be communications exchanged by people inside the Chinese Consulate on E. Erie Street and factions in both the Southside and Northside Chinatown's.

They were familiar with the business leaders from the two Chinatown's that had attended the dinner party on N. Astor Street and were somewhat suspicious of each of them. However, as of that time, they had no evidence that either Lily Mai Tong or Herbert Long were engaged in any illegal activities.

I picked up the check for our new team members and Elaina even though Henry Chan had offered to get it." You can get the next one." I said as we walked out onto Argyle Street. On the sidewalk I stopped dead in my tracks. Just a few doors down the block, I spotted a familiar menacing face. It was the large scowling man

41

from the Chinese Consulate. He was standing outside a nearby Chinese restaurant that Henry Chan knew to be owned by Herbert long. Henry pulled me and Elaina aside and whispered that he was familiar with the menacing man. His name was Yi Peng. Just then another Asian man of average size and middle-age exited the restaurant and approached Yi Peng and engaged him in what seemed to be an intense conversation.

Henry Chan turned his back to the pair and quietly said, "Get in your car. I've got an idea." We got into our Impala and Henry got into the driver's side of their car.

Teresa Marek walked away from us for a while pretending to look at menus on the outside of a couple of restaurants and gift shops. She then turned around and strolled back toward the two men still talking on the sidewalk. She stopped next door to them and lingered for a couple of minutes and then went right to them and said something to Herbert Long who seemed to laugh and nodded and pointed to a menu that she then stood reading for a few minutes.

Eventually the men ended their conversation and parted ways. Herbert Long went back into his restaurant and Yi Peng got into a black Toyota van in the passenger's seat joining a driver who was a slightly built young Asian man dressed in all black and they drove off.

I looked at Elaina and said that I would love to know what that was all about. As I did, Henry Chan walked over to the driver's side of our car and leaned in.

"Let's get out of this neighborhood before we become too obvious." I agreed and told him to meet us back at the station on North Latrobe. It was almost time for our team meeting anyway

Chapter 5

Back at the station Elaina and I arrived just ahead of our new FBI partners. We walked in together, and the rest of the team was already at their desks. I could tell by the look on their faces that they had not been informed of the FBI's involvement.

I proceeded to introduce special agents, Henry Chan and Teresa Marek. Everyone responded positively and welcomed them except, of course, Frank Kozlowski, who just mumbled something with his usual perturbed look on his face. It didn't seem to bother Marek and Chan. They probably expected a chillier reception than they got.

I started the meeting by reporting on the shooting outside of the Chinese Consulate on E. Erie Street., and the narrow escape of the Deputy Consulate General, Fong Wu, who looked to be the intended target. I reviewed our mostly uneventful experience at the Consulate and our run-in with the menacing Yi Peng. I then turned the meeting over to our new teammates.

Henry Chan began by relating his Chicago history and familiarity with the Asian neighborhoods and especially the Southside Chinatown. He explained that even though he had grown up in Chinatown, he was not fluent in Chinese since his grandparents were the last in his family to speak Mandarin. He then noted that his partner, Teresa Marek, however, spoke fluent Mandarin and also had knowledge of other Chinese dialects and some Asian languages. He then asked her to take over.

Teresa began by thanking us for accepting them onto our team and said that they were there to help. She also repeated some of our earlier conversations about the FBI's concern over increased chatter between Asian gang factions in both Chinatown and the Little Saigon area on the North Side.

She went on to say that they had no hard evidence that the Chinese Trade Consulate is directly involved with any of the tongs or gangs. However, she did say that there have been communications coming from the Consulate to parties on both the North and South Side Chinese groups.

Agent Marek continued telling the team about how valuable the language skills of agents at the FBI have been in monitoring communications between Hispanic and Asian gangs, especially. As an example, she told of her ability to listen to a portion of the conversation between dinner guest Herbert Long and consulate official Yi Peng earlier that afternoon. She expressed regret that she only heard a small portion of their conversation, but it was enough to learn that they were on very friendly terms and that they were cooperating on some kind of venture. It was also clear that Herbert Long was concerned about the shooting that morning and the safety of Deputy Consulate General Fong Wu, and the whereabouts of the second Deputy Consulate General Li Qjang.

I thanked Agent Marek and asked Detective Zilene Baker to report on what she and Detective Kozlowski had learned so far.

Detective Baker reported that none of the dinner guests were available at their jobs on Sunday, so they concentrated on gathering as much information on them as possible. She started with the high-tech guests.

"Li Zen is the 60-year-old Director of international Operations for the Shanghai Power and Technology Company which has offices in New York, Los Angeles, and most recently Chicago. Their office here is in the Hancock Center, or should I say 360 Chicago. They are supposedly looking to acquire land in the city or western suburbs to build a new technology campus. We have not been able to identify a permanent residence. He was last known to have a suite of rooms at the Ambassador."

"Grace Tobin, age 45, is a local woman who went to New Trier High School, MIT, and Harvard Business School. She lives in

Wilmette and operates a large high-tech research facility near the Illinois Tech campus on the Near Southside. Her home phone is unlisted, so we will try her when they open tomorrow morning at her office. She has no criminal record and is married with two adolescent children."

"Harriet Bingham, the Chief Investment Banker at Chicago First Multinational Bank, is 43 years old and divorced with no children. She grew up in Atlanta and was educated at Duke, and has an MBA from Loyola of Chicago. She lives in Streeterville and also has a clean record. We have just started the background checks on all of our assigned targets, but nothing has popped up on her so far."

"Dominic Blasi is a 35-year-old man, who grew up locally in Brookfield and attended St. Joseph High School in Westchester. He played basketball and baseball and had scholarship offers in both sports but decided to take an academic scholarship to Notre Dame. He then got a scholarship at The Kellogg School of Management at Northwestern University, where he received an MBA. He now lives in River Forest with his wife and seven-year-old son. He had a DUI while at Notre Dame and something as a juvenile that has been sealed. We will call on him at his offices on W. Jackson Boulevard."

Zilene sat down, and I asked Detective Morgan Latner to fill us in on what he and Detective Sanchez had found out. He began by relaying that the people they were investigating also had businesses that were not open on Sundays and that they would follow up with them tomorrow. He stated that Harry Sachman, age 51, who is the chief purchasing agent for America's leading retailer Maxi-Mart has a corporate apartment downtown and also had nothing criminal on his record, but has a habit of racking up parking tickets in the City. He grew up in New York City and attended NYU for both undergraduate and a Master's Degree in International Business.

He next reported on Francine Vito, the 46-year-old president of North American Importers, whose main Chicago offices are at the Merchandise Mart. "She is from the Cleveland area and went to Ohio State before working her way up from an entry-level job at North American all the way to President as of two years ago. She is a divorced mother of three with all her kids now adults are living on their own. She has a disorderly charge from 15 years ago, but there is no record of a disposition. She lives in the south loop."

"We were able to reinterview several of the neighbors who gave statements the previous evening, including George Townsend. None of those interviewed conveyed any significantly new information, but George Townsend and a couple of other neighbors offered to let us see the video from their security cameras which we made arrangements to follow up on as soon as they get them ready for us."

Morgan Latner sat down, and I decided to conclude the meeting by asking everyone to keep plugging away at their assignments and scheduled another meeting for Monday at 5 PM.

By the time the other detectives had finished up what they were doing on their computers and phones, it was almost 7 PM after they departed. Elaina and I were left with only the FBI agents in the detective's room on this summer Sunday evening.

I noticed Henry and Teresa huddled in a corner of the room before Agent Chan broke away and walked over to my desk. "I have a suggestion, Detective Fallon," he began. "I think I know where we may be able to find Lily Mai Tong tonight. Are you interested?"

"Hell yeah!" I said enthusiastically. "What do you have in mind?"

Agent Chan smiled and continued. "I actually know Lily very well. We went to high school together at Senn. It was a popular place for many people in Chinatown to send their kids because of its diverse student body and relatively safe neighborhood in Rogers

46

Park. We usually went up there in groups on the Red Line and sometimes carpooled. When we got to our junior and senior years, she was part of my travel group of friends, but we didn't hang out socially. She was a dancer doing modern and traditional Chinese dance, and I played soccer. She also ran with a little faster crowd than I did, if you know what I mean?"

"We run into each other occasionally in the old neighborhood, and of course, she has become very successful and is a significant presence in Chinatown. There is a very good chance that she will be at one of her karaoke clubs tonight. Probably the most successful one called East Asian Sounds on South Wentworth. I think it might be worth our while to check it out."

I was starting to get excited. We needed to get more information directly from the guests at the party. There was no reason to wait. "Okay, let's go for it." I exclaimed.

Henry Chan said that was great, but we didn't need to get there before 9:30 or 10.

Elaina stood up and said, "That sounds good to me. That gives us time to get something to eat. I'm starving."

Teresa Marek seconded that motion, and I said that I could go for some deep dish." How about ...." and before I could get it out, it seemed like everyone else said, "Pequods" at the same time. We all laughed. "I guess that settles that. Apparently, I don't need to tell anyone how to get there."

Outside we piled into our respective cars and found our way to the unassuming storefront super pizza parlor known for its caramelized crusted deep-dish pizza on North Clybourn Avenue called Pequod's.

After finding street parking about a block away, we walked in together into a bustling neighborhood pizza joint that has become a kind of poorly kept secret with a city and suburban wide following. We were seated at one of two open tables remaining and were quickly provided menus and ice waters. We ordered some soft drinks and ice teas and discussed the possible selections from a wide variety of toppings for deep-dish pizza. After a spirited debate, we settled on two medium pizzas, one with sausage, onions, and mushrooms, and the other with pepperoni, anchovies and black olives.

We had plenty of time which was good because the made-to-order pizzas at Pequods take a while. We took the time to get to know each other a little bit better during the wait throughout the delicious pizza meal. By the time we were finished, it was nearly 9:30 and time to head to Chinatown.

There was fairly heavy traffic in the City, and we got separated from the Agents, but we were heading to Elaina's home territory as Pilsen and Chinatown were neighboring areas on the Near Southside. Of course, this was agent Chan's home base even more. Hence, it wasn't surprising that after we found a spot in the 2200 block of S. Wentworth Avenue, not far from the Chinatown Gate at the corner of Wentworth; Cermak Chan and Marek were already waiting for us outside of the East Asian Sounds nightclub.

We met up, and Agent Chan led the way into the nondescript building and up some dimly lit stairs to a landing, where two serious-looking young men dressed in cream-colored silk suit coats and black linen pants were manning the entrance to the club. They weren't interested in checking our IDs but ordered us to stop and started to frisk Agent Chan. He subtly pulled one of the man's hands away from his Glock 9 mm and showed him his FBI credentials, as did Teresa Marek. Elaina and I simply exposed the Stars on our belts.

The other young man whispered something to the first one and disappeared into the club. A minute later, he returned and waved us into the dark main bar room, which was lighted only by some neon panels in the walls, tables, bar and floor. My senses were temporarily overloaded by the cornucopia of colors with a variety of blue, red, green and yellow hues. The room was moderately busy, which Henry Chan said would change to a much larger crowd later.

We asked for a table and were ushered over to a four-top in a corner of the large space, which included a small stage, a couple of VIP sections with couches, tables, etc. and a large bar lit up by two neon ribbons running along the top and bottom of the long glass-topped counter. I could see that there were some private rooms, but there didn't seem to be anything going on in them at the time.

An attractive young woman dressed in a white button-down short-sleeved blouse and a very short Navy-blue skirt came over to get our drink order, and Henry said that he would order for us. She took the order, and we turned our attention to the business at hand. Without being obvious, Agent Chan informed us that our person of interest, Lily Mai Tong, was sitting on a couch in one of the VIP sections with several other people and flanked by a couple of unmistakable bodyguard types.

At that moment, Lily Mai looked up directly at our table. I thought I detected a slight smile which quickly evaporated into a calm but commanding expression.

Our drinks were delivered, and each one was a different color served in a tall cylindrical glass. Mine was orange and red, looking like a tequila sunrise not as sweet and definitely not containing tequila. The other drinks were blue, yellow and pink and were also devoid of alcohol.

As we tasted our colorful kiddie cocktails, I noticed Lily Mai get up from the couch and walk directly toward us, crossing the dance floor. She was dressed in a black sleeveless, incredibly revealing dress with slits on both sides of her shapely hips running all the way down to the floor. She seemed to glide on top of her black sandals and her every move was mesmerizing. She arrived at our table and simply stood there looking at us with her deep dark brown eyes. It was breathtaking.

"Henry, how are you, my dear. It has been too long."

"I am well, Lily," he replied. "How are things going for you?"

Lily answered that things were good and getting better but still recovering a little from the COVID. She said hello to Teresa Marek and seemed to have met her previously.

"Are you going to introduce me to your friends?" She asked as she looked directly at me. I have to admit she was an exciting woman, and I felt it. Henry made the introductions, and she offered her hand briefly to Elaina and then pressed her small, soft, and intensely warm hand into mine and left it there for what seemed like an unusually long time, but I didn't want it to end.

Eventually, Elaina decided to snap me out of it and asked Lily if we could talk to her about what happened at the dinner party the night before. Lily gently and slowly slid her hand out of mine and continued looking at me for a moment before turning to Elaina. "Oh yes, very unfortunate. Very unfortunate. I will be most happy to talk to you about that but not tonight. I have a very important business meeting in a few minutes. It will have to be another time."

I reached into my wallet and grabbed my card, and offered it to her. She accepted it from me and glanced at it before saying, "I will be in touch with you, Detective Jack Fallon." And she added that it was nice to meet Elaina and to see Henry and Teresa again before turning and walking elegantly back to her VIP couch.

As soon as Lily Mai sat down, the lights under the small dance floor began flashing and pulsating with the music, which was unidentifiable to me but definitely Oriental. The sound raised a couple of decibel levels. An announcement was made that karaoke was available upon request, and drink specials were served until midnight.

As if on cue, people started coming in, and the place began filling up and becoming more lively. Through the crowd, I spotted something that caused the hair on my neck and arms to stand on end. It was the ominous presence of Yi Peng. He walked in by himself, and as he approached, several people who were sitting with Lily Mai abruptly stood up and departed the VIP section. Only Lily and Yi Peng remained other than her bodyguards, who visibly tensed up and moved closer to her when Yi Peng sat down next to her.

Everyone at our table saw the same thing and was fixated on what was transpiring in the VIP section. Teresa whispered that she would love to get closer to listen to their conversation, but that looked to be impossible. Due to the high decibel level of the music, she would have to be sitting right next to them to hear anything. All we could do was watch and wait.

After only a few minutes, the meeting ended. Yi Peng stood up and walked away with what seemed to be an even more menacing scowl on his face, if that was possible. He walked across the now more crowded dance floor, brushing aside anyone who did not get out of his way. Lily's bodyguards backed up a little, and one of the men that had been sitting with Lily previously, approached and bent down close to Lily. She leaned forward toward him and said something that caused him to stand up straight with a concerned look on his face and briskly walk away.

We discussed following the guy, but it would have been obvious, and we still wanted to have information from Lily Mai Tong. So, we decided to stay and see what happens next.

What happened next didn't take long. There were muffled sounds of something happening near the door, but whatever it was, only lasted for a couple of seconds and didn't seem alarming. What followed was more than alarming.

Three young Asian men walked into the club and casually went directly toward the VIP section and Lily Mai. Her bodyguards didn't notice them until they were only about 10 feet away, and one of them stepped out in front of Lily, as did the man she had just spoken with.

I could feel and see the danger. We needed to act. Now! I stood up and told agents Chan and Marek to clear the dance floor. Just as I did, the three men drew guns from under their light-colored sport coats and opened fire. The first bodyguard and the other man were hit with the first volley and went down. The second bodyguard covered Lily Mai with his body as the sea of people on the dance floor was parted by Chan and Marek. Elaina and I opened fire, and two of the assassins went down. The third guy kept firing and hitting the courageous bodyguard, still draping his body over Lily. Elaina and I fired another round of shots, and the third assassin was spun around and actually fell onto the pulsating dance floor face first, looking painfully right at us.

In a matter of one minute, it was over. Everything still seemed to be moving in slow motion, and the now smoke-filled atmosphere at The East Asian sounds club became even more surreal.

I called dispatch for backup and several ambulances. I then rushed over to Lily and literally had to lift her bodyguard off of her and placed him gently onto the couch next to her. She immediately attempted to give aid to her loyal protector by tearing off part of her dress and trying to stop his bleeding, but there were multiple gunshot wounds that needed attention. I took off my coat and used it to compress blood loss coming from his stomach. He was alive and making some gurgling noises, but I knew he didn't have long. Elaina, Henry and Teresa were attending to the other victims and the assailants. Only one of the assailants was still alive, and he was just barely holding on.

It only took a few minutes for Officers and EMTs to start pouring into the club, but it seemed much longer. They were directed to those that were still breathing and started hooking them up to intravenous tubes and bags of different solutions, including what I assumed was plasma. When they took the bodyguard out on a gurney, Lily Mai insisted on going with him. She wouldn't take no for an answer, and when they looked at me for direction, I just nodded and said, "Let her go with him." Lily looked up at me

52

sorrowfully and said, "Thank you, Detective Fallon. You saved my life. I owe you. I will be in touch when I can." And off they went down the stairs and into the warm summer Chicago night

Chapter 6

The Dawn on Monday began when the alarm on my phone chimed in at 6:30, and I awoke from four hours of deep but inadequate sleep. The vague memory of my birthday only two days before seemed like ancient history. It was Monday. I was reasonably sure of that. My days were now going to blend together into one continuum of time until this case came to a conclusion one way or the other.

We had stayed at the club in Chinatown until around 2 AM, and some of the images from what happened there were still fresh in my mind and still troubling. When the dust settled inside East Asian Sounds, we discovered the two doormen in the hallway outside the front door, both laid out on the floor propped up against the wall. One had a knife sticking out of his neck, and the other had one planted directly into his chest. It was a bloody mess, and the look on their faces continued to haunt me.

I popped out of bed looked out of the living room windows onto a bright summer day. Next, I went to the bathroom to take care of my morning ritual. The swelling on my left temple had largely receded and no longer throbbed and my black eye was now a thin yellow ribbon. I felt a powerful urge to fix myself a big breakfast which was not typically part of my morning routine. It occurred to me that I hadn't eaten since we had pizza the previous evening at Pequods. For whatever reason, I was ravenous.

I got started by mixing three eggs with a bit of half-and-half and some Cholula hot sauce into a mixture ready for making scrambled eggs. I put five slices of bacon on my cast-iron frypan, and a couple of slices of Catherine Clark wheat bread into the toaster. I was ready to execute one of my favorite breakfasts.

While cooking, I listened to phone messages from my dad Ed and sister, Molly, who had both heard about the incidents on N.

Astor St. at the Chinese Consulate and in Chinatown. Apparently, the media was now fully onto this case, and my name was being mentioned on the news. I wasn't happy to learn that. It was just another annoying thing to deal with. I was also informed by my dad that the weather had turned and was likely to be hot and humid for the next few days. Not my favorite working weather.

While eating the eggs, crispy bacon and toasted wheat bread with strawberry jam accompanied by chocolate milk, I noticed that I had texts for my brother Barry and friends and fellow Detectives, Morgan Latner and Ricky Del Signore, who were checking to make sure I was okay. I shot all of them a quick text, assuring them that I was fine and telling Latner that I would see him at the team meeting today at 5 PM.

I expected to have a morning filled with interviews and reports regarding the shooting at the club. Elaina and I had our guns confiscated by the detectives who interviewed us on the scene, and I knew that we would have to meet with internal Affairs as well as sitting for mandatory psychological evaluations. It was a real pain, and I was desperately trying to figure out a way to avoid administrative duty.

I checked in with my partner, Elaina Rodriguez before getting into my black-on-black Chevy Camaro and getting on Lakeshore Drive heading south. It was already getting hot and muggy, and even dressed in a short-sleeve shirt with a lightweight cotton sport coat and summer slacks, I felt vastly overdressed. When I arrived at the station around 8:15 AM, I spotted Elaina's Jeep and the Ford driven by our FBI teammates. When I walked into the detective's room, I was met by Lieutenant Tyrone Whitehead, who was sitting down near Elaina, Henry and Teresa.

Whitehead asked me to sit down and spoke to us in a calm but serious tone. "We have one helluva fucking situation here. The Chinese Consulate is demanding the body of their Consulate General and the bodies of the three assassins who were killed in

Chinatown last night. I don't know what the hell is going on. As you all know, the shooters had no ID on them, and the FBI took their prints, and nothing showed up on any known database. What in the hell?"

"We are getting calls from the Justice Department and representatives from our two Senators and several Congressmen and Congresswomen. "Agents Chan and Marek, I'm hoping you can handle some of these calls." They both nodded, and Agent Chan said that they would be happy to do so.

Whitehead went on to say that Elaina and I would be busy with the investigation into the last night's shooting much of the morning, so Chan and Marek would handle the federal level calls and report any problems to him. He was adamant that he wanted our investigation to proceed rapidly and had already made a request to our District Commander, to try to speed up the Internal Affairs process. "If ever I have heard of a good shoot, last night was one. Now let's get going."

Whitehead got up and left the room, and we got busy on our computers and phones. I got in touch with our other teammates who were already out in the field on their way to interview their various persons of interest. I informed them about what happened in Chinatown the night before and told them that Elaina and I would be caught up in the Internal Affairs investigation for much of the morning, but after that, we would gather the autopsy reports and any updates from the witnesses from The East Asian Sounds Club and re-interviews with Prof. Borland and Curator Carlisle.

At that time, Agents Chan and Marek announced that they had been ordered back to their FBI offices for a debriefing on the shootings at the club. Their process was different than ours, and because they had not fired their weapons, they didn't have to surrender them. They expected to be back before noon.

Elaina and I soon started the CPD protocol with Internal Affairs interviewing me first and the department psychologist taking Elaina. About an hour later, we switched places. By around 11:30, we were done. We both felt like the Internal Affairs Officers were satisfied that we would be found to have acted properly. On the other hand, the psychologist gave us both the impression that she was on the verge of discovering something terribly wrong with us but just didn't have the time to determine exactly what it was, so she was going to give us a pass.

Our FBI friends weren't back yet, so Elaina and I decided to get on our phones and contact our art experts and the Crime Scene Team. I started with Belinda Carlisle and Elaina took Prof. Borland; since we had each interviewed the other one on Saturday night.

I called the Art Institute, and after being transferred three times, I heard a voice say, "This is Curator Belinda Chin Carlisle." I identified myself, and there was a long pause before she spoke again. "How can I help you, Detective?" She said in a low unenthusiastic voice.

"Thank you for taking the time to speak to me." I replied. "I wanted to check in to see how you are doing."

She paused again before saying that, as I might have expected, she was miserable and overwhelmed with guilt about losing the Egg of Chaos. She went on to say, "We are totally at a loss on what to do. We are so hoping that you can help us. Will you promise to do that? Will you promise to find the Egg of Chaos?" She pleaded.

I could sense the desperation in her voice, and it moved me. "I promise Belinda. I promise not to stop until I get it back for you." I said as convincingly as I knew how; even though deep down I knew it might be impossible, I felt that she needed to hear me say it.

I asked her to give me as much information as possible that could help me find her precious artifact. She gave me some of the background, which included that it was definitely from the early Han dynasty and probably from the first century BCE since the white jade used along with the green jade was only discovered

57

during the first century BCE in central Asia. It was usually kept at the Imperial Palace Museum within the Forbidden City. It is priceless and, as far as she knew, a unique, absolutely one-of-a-kind piece.

I asked her where someone could go to sell something like the Egg, and she didn't think that it would be possible at any of the legitimate auction houses in New York or London or anywhere else. She thought that it might be possible to sell it on the black market, but even there, it would be difficult to keep quiet.

We talked for a while longer, but she didn't have much information that was useful since she had left the townhouse right away after the smoke bombs went off before returning, when Elaina interviewed her, and she really didn't know any of the other guests other than Professor Borland. She said that she had been contacted by an assistant to the Deputy Consulate General Fong Wu to arrange for the private showing, and they only met when she arrived at the townhouse early on Saturday night.

I thanked her again and sincerely asked her not to blame herself and to take the weight off her shoulders. We would do our best to get the Egg of Chaos back to the Art Institute. She thanked me and said, "I believe you will. I trust you, Detective Fallon."

My next call was to the Medical Examiner's Office while Elaina decided to contact the CSI team. Her conversation with Prof. Nils Borland wasn't very enlightening or noteworthy, except that Elaina noticed his uncertainty about precisely what he had done immediately after the smoke bombs went off and how long it took him to exit the house.

I dialed up the ME's Office and was happy to learn that Dr. Gorman was available. She had worked personally on the unidentified young woman and had access to the report on Consulate General Zhao Chen. She started with the young woman and stated that the autopsy had not revealed who she was, of course, but it did give us some indications about who she was not. Dr.

Gorman explained that the young woman was of Asian descent, but her dental work strongly suggested that she grew up in the United States or possibly Canada. She was almost certainly not a Chinese national.

The cause of her death was respiratory failure due to a massive overdose of heroin. However, her organs were exceptionally healthy, and there was no outward indication of repeated heroin use. There were no signs of collapsed veins, bacterial infections of blood vessels, soft tissue infections, or multiple needle marks. In fact, she had found only one injection point. This indicated to her that she was administered one massive dose which caused her lungs to seize up. "Somebody gave her one hell of a hotshot."

"She seems to have been in her mid-20s to about 30 years old and, as I said, was in excellent health before the overdose. There are no signs of smoking damage or any damage to her liver. There was no alcohol or drugs in her bloodstream other than the heroin. We checked her body for fingerprints and DNA, but we didn't detect anything useful."

"Now, let's take a look at the autopsy report prepared by Dr. Paez," she said, "just a minute, I have it right here. Okay. The cause of death here is as obvious as it looks. He was killed by the 357 bullet in his forehead, which was fired from very close range, as indicated by the heavy gun powder residue and some burn marks on his face and forehead. The manner of death is homicide for both of the victims. There was no gun found at the scene or shell casings, so it was likely a revolver or a four-barrel derringer. The Consulate General had a generous amount of alcohol and a very recent meal of Peking duck, rice, and vegetables in his stomach. His last meal was fit for a king."

"I signed off with the ME's office just as Elaina finished her call with the CSI team. As it turned out, there wasn't a lot to report from CSI. They thoroughly searched the entire townhouse and did not find any other smoke bomb canisters, so it looked like the four they found on Saturday night; were the only ones. There were no shell casings, no blood other than a small amount on the Council General's desk. The 357 slug in the forehead had plugged up the wound and prevented the excessive bleeding typically associated with head wounds. There were hundreds of fingerprints all over the house and on glasses, plates and silverware. The two upstairs floors were vacuumed, and the contents will be checked for possible DNA, but it would be a while it was unlikely to produce any useful information."

While Elaina and I were finishing our exchange of information, Agents Chan and Marek walked into the detective's room, almost immediately followed by Lieutenant. Whitehead looking for an update. I summed up what we had learned from the ME and CSI, and Agent Marek relayed that she and Agent Chan were thoroughly debriefed at FBI headquarters, and they had been ordered to continue working with us. They were also told to promise full cooperation from the FBI. They had already begun trying to determine the identities of the three shooters from The East Asian Sounds Club, and looking into any intelligence intercepts that might relate to the Chinese Consulate and Chinese communities in Chicago.

Whitehead took it all in and said that he wanted to be kept in the loop. He turned to walk out of the room but then turned back and said, "I am still pushing the brass to get Internal Affairs to move quickly on clearing you two to get you back on full duty, but it will probably be at least another day."

Agent Chan interjected that he had an idea about a temporary solution to our situation. He said that he had discussed this issue with his Supervising Agent, and he suggested that Detectives Fallon and Rodriguez could work for a few days under the auspices of the FBI. They couldn't provide the detectives with guns by it would allow them to get out of the Station.

Whitehead didn't respond for a minute. It was clear that he was considering the idea when his cell phone rang. He said, "Okay. Thanks. I'll get back to you." His voice sounded grave when he spoke. "Harry Sachman, the head purchasing agent for Maxi-Mart and one of our dinner guests, was just gunned down on North Michigan. That settles it." He exclaimed. I want you to respond to this right now. I'll clear it with Internal Affairs. Don't make me regret this, Fallon."

And off we went.

Chapter 7

We climbed into our green Impala, and the agents drove off in a blue Ford sedan. Within a few minutes, we were pulling up to a full-blown crime scene on the east side of the 600 block of N. Michigan Ave. Morgan Latner and Henrique Sanchez were already there and taking charge. Uniformed officers were scurrying around directing traffic and taping off the sidewalk, and the media was starting to arrive. Wonderful.

Once on the sidewalk, I could see the body of a middle-aged man wearing what appeared to be an expensive cream-colored suit. He was face down with a fresh pool of blood, still oozing from an obvious wound to his left temple.

I approached Detective Latner who was finishing a conversation with a uniformed officer. When he turned from her and spotted me, he walked directly to me. "What have we got here, Morgan?" I asked. He answered that he was not on the scene when it happened but that witnesses have all said that a couple of guys drove up on motorcycles dressed in black and full visor helmets. They came to an abrupt stop, hopped off their bikes and pulled pistols with long barrels, and opened fire on our victim here. We found some shell casings and believe that the shooters were using silencers because none of the witnesses reported hearing loud shots. What they heard was more of a popping than a banging.

"Has the victim been positively identified?" I wanted to know. Detective Sanchez responded that he was without a doubt one of our people of interest, Harry Sachman. He had his ID on him, and Detectives Sanchez and Latner had just finished interviewing him earlier that morning at one Prudential Plaza. He mentioned that he had an appointment to meet with Deputy Consulate General Li Qjang Yong at the Consulate on E. Erie Street later that morning. The Consulate was just a couple of blocks from there.

"Did he mention what the meeting was about?" I asked. Morgan nodded and replied that Sachman had stated that doing business with the Chinese was getting more complicated all of a sudden and that he had hoped some questions might get answered at the dinner party but that the smoke alarms went off before the more serious discussions got underway. So, he was expecting to get some answers this morning. "I'm sure this wasn't the answer he was looking for."

"I think we need to get back over to the consulate. It seemed like everyone who attended their little dinner party is a target right now. We need to figure out why."

I huddled with Elaina and the special agents and relayed the information from Detective Latner. Everyone found the timing of the attacks to be highly alarming and that going back to the consulate was a good idea.

We took the short drive to one E. Erie and entered the building. We showed our identification and were told to go up to the consulate. Exiting the elevator on the fifth floor, we entered the waiting room and encountered a couple of uniformed sentries and once again showed our IDs and asked to see either of the Deputy Consulate Generals. One of the guards went into the consulate and then returned accompanied by Deputy General Li Qjang Yong, a tall, slender but athletic-looking man, who appeared to be in his early 40s and another shorter Asian man with gray hair who looked to be about 60. They exchanged some words in Chinese, and the shorter man departed.

Li Yong smiled and invited us into his office within the consulate, which was just closing up for the day. Deputy Consulate General Fong Wu and her scary-looking assistant Yi Peng were nowhere to be seen.

We followed Yong into his spacious office and sat down in comfortable leather chairs as the Deputy General settled into his oversized executive chair behind a beautiful mahogany desk.

"How may I help you detectives, or should I say, agents?" He smiled broadly as if he had said something very clever. We all looked at each other and decided to play along, and chuckled. I took the lead and said that Elaina and I were detectives and Teresa and Henry were special agents, but whatever terms he wanted to use were fine with us.

"First, we would like to convey our condolences concerning the loss of your Consulate General, Zhao Chen. Li Yong bowed his head a little and said that he sincerely thanked us." He was a very great man. This is very shocking, very shocking."

I asked him to go over the events of the evening of the dinner party, and he informed us that there was nothing unusual or that contradicted what other witnesses had said. He thought everything was going very well up until the moment the smoke bombs went off.

He explained that he and Fong Wu were in the study with Zhao Chen, and the last of the visitors to see the unique artwork had just gone back downstairs. Then the bombs went off, and General Chen ordered us to go and help the guests and staff get out of the building. He would collect the Egg of Chaos and some official papers and follow us out. He told his security guards to assist us, and we went down the smoke-filled stairs. Once at the bottom, we began helping people out of the dining room and then down the steps to the sidewalk. Visibility was terrible; even outside was filled with heavy smoke.

"I don't know how long it was, but when the smoke began to clear outside, I noticed that Zhao Chen did not make it out of the house. So, I went back inside and made my way up the stairs and into the smoke-filled library and found the Consulate General looking like he did."

"Do you remember which of the guests the last to leave the study were?" I asked. "Yes." He replied. "It was Ms. Francine Vito from North American Imports and Mr. Harry Sachman from Maxi-

64

Mart. "They are significant importers of Chinese products. Yes. Very important."

"Speaking of Harry Sachman, I understand that you had a meeting scheduled with him this morning."

Li Yong looked surprised and nodded. "Yes, I did have a meeting scheduled with Mr. Sachman, but I got delayed dealing with an official call from Beijing, and Deputy Consulate General Fong Wu met with him instead.

"Is Deputy Wu available?" I inquired. Yong responded that she was no longer at the consulate after being called out to another meeting. However, he did have a question for us. He wanted to know when they could claim the body of Zhao Chen. He expressed that it was imperative his family be able to perform a traditional burial ceremony in China.

I promised the Deputy that we would check on releasing the body as soon as possible, and he thanked us. Before we left, I had one last question for him. "Do you know this woman?"

I then showed him a picture of the young woman found in one of the upper floor bedrooms at the townhouse. He said that he did not recognize her but that she appeared to be wearing the same shirt that servers from the catering business that worked the dinner, were wearing. He would check on who they hired to do the catering and get back to us. We thanked him for his time, and he walked us to the door. I handed him my card, and we were then headed back to the elevators.

When we got to the street, Agents Marek and Chan walked with Elaina and me to our car and asked if they could join us for a minute. I looked at Elaina, and she nodded, and I said *sure*. We all climbed into our car and waited for someone to initiate the conversation.

After a couple of seconds, Teresa Marek spoke up. "Some things are going on here that we have decided to share with you because they may be connected to the murders on North Astor Street on Saturday and what happened last night in Chinatown. It is not clear to us whether Harry Sachman's murder is related, but because he was at the dinner party Saturday night, we have to assume that it may be.

We have been monitoring communications as we normally do throughout the United States, that could be connected to a wide range of criminal activity as well as domestic and foreign terrorism and espionage. In recent weeks something dramatically changed about the communications coming out of the Chinese Trade Consulate here in Chicago and some of its officials. For the first time that we are aware of, there have been frequent exchanges between some of Chicago's Latin gangs and in particular Mexican gangs that are known to be large movers of heroin here.

Elaina and I were somewhat floored by this revelation. Elaina excitedly uttered, "Mio Dios. I have never heard of anything like that in Pilsen or Little Village. It seems so unlikely."

"We thought so too." Henry Chan chimed in. "It didn't make sense, but we decided to focus on the consulate and known Asian gangs in Chinatown and Little Saigon. To our surprise, we picked up a lot of chatter going back and forth among the Asian gangs and some factions of the Latin gangs and consulate officials. We didn't have warrants to listen to the conversation, so we could only monitor the frequency and phone numbers involved. We are working on getting the authority for wiretaps."

"What is really strange about this, "Agent Marek explained, is that while the Latin gangs have been involved in heroin distribution in Chicago, the Asian gangs have not been involved in any significant way. And even though opium has a long history in China and there has been usage of opium among groups of Chinese-Americans, it has primarily been smoked and has faded somewhat with younger Chinese-Americans.

Consequently, we decided to place one of our young female agents into one of the catering businesses on Argyle Street. It turned out that she was hired by a business, owned by one of the dinner guests, Herbert Long, who we now know is an acquaintance of the menacing-looking Yi Peng.

"We thought we hit a home run when our agent was asked to help cater the party hosted by the consulate at the townhouse on North Astor Street. She has a Vietnamese American mother and a Chinese-American father and grew up mainly in New York City's Chinatown. She had worked in restaurants in Chinatown and had a passing knowledge of Mandarin. Her name is or was Kira Vu Sing. Obviously, her death has hit us hard. She was only 27 years old."

"In the days leading up to the dinner party, she reported seeing a number of well-dressed Asian men coming into the restaurant, which wasn't unusual in itself, but there were also many young Latino men coming in, which was unusual. She wasn't able to overhear any of their conversations, but she had been impressed by the serious looks of the Asians and the hyper vigilant behavior of the Latinos."

"One other thing," Teresa Marek added, "when we were going into the consulate today, I overheard a little of the parting conversation between Deputy General Yong and the official from Shanghai Power, Li Zen. They spoke with a dialect that is common in Shanghai and other cities in Jiangsu and Zhejiang Provinces. The content was just small talk and didn't mean much to me, but it reminded me of what I heard from one of the shooters at the nightclub in Chinatown. He was ordering the other two to kill the woman just before all hell broke loose. He spoke in the same Wu dialect or commonly referred to as Shanghainese. It didn't register with me then, but after hearing the Deputy General Yong speaking it, I thought it could be relevant."

"Wow!" Was all I could think and say at first. "This really could change everything. But why this odd couple's dinner party with a private showing of an invaluable Chinese artifact, and why go after the consulate officials and guests at this dinner party? If this was just a high-end professional robbery, why keep going? They already have the Egg!"

"That's too many questions to answer all at once, Jack." Elaina responded. "I think we should pursue the heroin angle and the Latin gang involvement. I still have some contacts in the Southside gang units and on the street in Pilsen. I know a great place for lunch. Follow us down to Cantina Maria on W. 18th Street." she said, looking at Agents Chan and Marek.

Henry Chan said that he knew the place, and in a few moments, we were on our way to Pilsen.

Elaina decided to take the scenic route down Halsted Street through Greektown and then south of Roosevelt road, I began to notice things change. My eyes lit up at the site of incredibly colorful murals of striking, beautiful faces of women, men and children, along with creative artwork of many colorful types. I didn't know what a lot of it was, but it was all fantastic!

The streets were full of people bustling about shopping from street vendors and stopping to listen to musicians playing violins, accordions, guitars, drums and some instruments I didn't recognize. I felt a little ashamed that I had never experienced this wonderful part of Chicago before.

The sweltering heat didn't deter the people of Pilsen at all. In fact, it seemed to bring them out in celebration on this sizzling sunny summer day in this culturally wealthy neighborhood in the great City of Chicago. We passed through the impressive middle European architecture, built by the Czechs and Germans who moved into the neighborhood in droves in the late 1800s and which was now populated mainly by Mexican Americans who added their musical, artistic and culinary culture to this thriving place. I knew some of the history of Pilsen from my grandfather, whose grandparents had settled in Pilsen in the 1840s along with other Irish immigrants fleeing Ireland during the great famine.

I broke away from my hypnotic gaze at the neighborhood and noticed a look of pride and joy on Elaina's face that made me smile. "Now I know why you said I should come to Pilsen," I said admiringly. "I can't believe that I have somehow missed out on this place my whole life. I didn't think that I could love this City any more, but then I see all this."

"Thanks, Jack." she said, grinning from ear-to-ear. "I grew up feeling the same way. We have our problems here, to be sure, but the vast majority of people in this community are hard-working, good people. The gangs are here, and they tend to give everyone a bad name. It isn't fair, but it is a reality. That's life."

We got to 18th St. and turned right going west, and the activity on the streets continued to mesmerize me until we arrived in front of Cantina Maria Mexican food restaurant.

We walked into the cozy rustic neighborhood restaurant, and a smiling middle-aged woman with long brown hair and sparkling Hazel eyes immediately approached us and entered into a warm embrace with my partner. They exchanged greetings and a few sentences in Spanish, and then the smiling lady who clearly held a prominent position there turned to the rest of us and said, "I am Maria. You're all welcome con mucho gusto! Please sit here." And she showed us to a large table in the back.

"You will have some privacy here. All friends of Elaina are our friends as well." She went on to ask Elaina how her children Rosie and Lucy were doing and then asked about her husband, Paco. While being assured that they were all well, she asked what she could get us to drink. When no one immediately responded, she said, "Have the fresh-squeezed lemonade. It is just the thing for a hot day."

We all looked at each other, and I said, "Absolutely! We'll have four lemonades."

The ice-cold drinks arrived right away with menus, and we refocused on our primary reason for being there. On the way to Pilsen, Elaina made a few phone calls and got in touch with contacts in the lower Westside and Near Southside gang units, and reached out to a confidential informant that she had known for several years. She expected that a couple of Gang Unit Detectives would meet us at the restaurant, and she was waiting to hear back from her CI after leaving a message.

Elaina ordered four small plates of food for us to share, and before we had time to exchange ideas about our daunting and very convoluted case, her phone buzzed. It was her informant, and she said, "Okay. Okay. Si." She hung up and said, "He wants to meet me right now at Benito Juarez Park. Jack, I am going to take the car."

I just looked at Elaina for a moment. I didn't like the idea of her going to the park by herself, and I suggested that I should go with her. "No, it would spook him and possibly draw some unwanted attention." I yielded to her wishes, but I made her promise that if anything didn't look or feel right, she would get the hell out of there. She just smiled at me and said, "Okay, poppy."

Soon after she left, the food was brought out along with refills of the best lemonade I've ever tasted. Just as we started to enjoy the sumptuous meal of various hopes and tacos, melted cheeses and a variety of tortilla chips with guacamole.

My attention turned to the front door as two imposingly large men entered the restaurant and walked straight toward us. I could see that Agents Marek and Chan were experiencing the same reaction. They sat upright and instinctively put their hands on their 9 mm weapons.

The men slowed their approach and looked at each other laughing. "Relax guys. Didn't Elaina tell you we were coming?" Said the dark-haired swarthy man of about 38 years. My eyes went to their belts, where their holsters and Stars, now, were plainly visible and very welcome.

I relaxed and let out, "Sorry, fellas, we are a little edgy today. Yes, Elaina mentioned that you might come by. Please sit down and join us. They introduced themselves as Detectives José Santos and Devin Bulger of the Lower Westside Gang Unit. After completing our introductions, I explained that my partner Elaina had gone to the park to meet with a CI.

"Did you send anyone with her?" Detective Bulger asked.

I responded that she wouldn't let me go with her, and they both laughed. "That's Elaina, all right." Detective Santos said, shaking his head. "She's very stubborn and fearless."

I asked them if they would like to have some food and lemonade, and they declined before waving over our waitress to the table. They ordered two Modelos beers, and I couldn't help but think that these two guys seemed to walk to a different drummer. They didn't wear coats, just short-sleeved white button-down shirts without ties. The waitress brought over two Modelos which the men seemed to inhale before ordering two more. Their thirst was impressive.

Before their next round arrived, my phone buzzed, and then so did Detective Santo's phone. My dispatcher informed me that there was a report of shots fired at the Benito Juarez Park called in by Detective Rodriguez and then they lost the call. I stood up and told Agents Chan and Marek that we needed to go right now. The detectives stood up. "And Santos said shots were fired at the park near the mural. Someone had been hit. That was all he knew."

"We'll take you there. Follow us."

My heart sank, and my mind raced and went into intense battle mode. It was amazing how quickly everyone sprang into action. I literally threw some bills onto the table without knowing what they were. I later realized that I was probably going to win tipper of the year.

We all ran out the door as Maria looked on in astonishment. She grasped the seriousness of the situation and yelled out something in Spanish that felt like it meant *good luck and be careful.*

I jumped into the backseat behind Henry and Teresa, and we raced off right behind Santos and Bulger, who pulled out in front of us and charged down 18th St. with blue lights flashing and their siren blowing. Cars and trucks began pulling over, and they weaved skillfully through the traffic that was slow to get out of the way with us right behind. They turned down South Laflin Street, and we were in close pursuit. In moments we came upon the wide-open city park populated by what looked to be at least a dozen statues.

The detective's car suddenly jumped the curb and took off across the lawns and sidewalks.

Henry Chan looked back at me quizzically, and I yelled, "Go! Don't stop!"

We bounced, then flew over the curb and came down with a jolt that rattled my teeth. The detectives didn't slow down and headed directly toward a prominent statue and colorful mural. They came to a sudden stop, which caused their card to swerve on the grass and go into a 90° tailspin. We stopped right behind them, and everyone jumped out.

Detectives Santos and Bulger had their guns drawn. Agents Marek and Chan had their hands on theirs which were still holstered. I didn't have to decide what to do with mine. It was in the possession of Internal Affairs. We were the first ones to respond.

Just to the left of the detective's car Elaina Rodriguez sat on the grass holding the bleeding head of a young Latino man. She was rocking him in her arms and silently sobbing with tears streaming down her pain-stricken face. It was the most profound expression of deep sorrow and despair that I have ever witnessed.

Detective Santos approached her with surprising calm and gentleness. He whispered something to her in Spanish, which caused her sobs to pour out violently and then evolve into one loud, long primordial scream. Santos sat down beside her and wrapped his powerful arms around her as she continued to hold the young man's head in her hands. He was gone, but the pain and power of the moment lived on. I allowed myself to wonder whether this needless cycle of violence and sacrificial killing of the young would ever end.

Chapter 8

After the park started clearing out and we finished giving our statements to the detectives from District 12 who responded to the scene, we parted ways with Detectives Santos and Bulger. I told Chan and Marek that we would see them back at our Station for the 5 pm meeting.

Elaina and I sauntered to our car, which she had parked nearby on Laflin Street, without speaking a word. At the car, she handed me the key fob and got into the passenger seat for the first time, again, without saying anything or looking directly at me. Once inside, we just sat there for a while. Finally, I said, "I'm okay with you not saying anything. I really am. But whenever you're ready........"

She let out a long sigh, and her eyes welled up, but she caught herself and began speaking. She then didn't stop until we got to the Station.

She told the story about how she met the young man named Chico about four years ago when he first contacted the District 12 Headquarters and asked to speak to a Latino detective. "I was the only one at the Station at the moment, so I took the call. He was an emotional wreck after finding his older sister Manuella dead on their kitchen floor. She had a bad reaction from shooting heroin and just stopped breathing. It was her first time using, and he was only 17 when he found her. He was furious and wanted to lash out at the gangs, at anyone that pushed the deadly shit in his neighborhood. He was still in high school and managed to stay out of the gangs, but he knew many of the Latin Kings and Latin Counts from Pilsen and Little Village. It was unavoidable. At first, he wanted to find a gun. He didn't have one and had never wanted one before. Now, he wanted to kill the first gang member he could find on the street. I could tell that he didn't really want to do that. It wasn't who he was.

But I sensed how real his anger was and was afraid that he might do something stupid. Maybe even kill someone or get himself killed. I told him about our relationship with confidential informants and how he could help get drugs off the streets and hurt the gangs more by providing information to us rather than ruining his life and bringing more sorrow to his parents by seeking revenge. He told me that he wasn't sure he could do it. He would get back to me."

She paused for a moment.

"Two months later, I got a call from Chico, and he was ready to help. I tell you, Jack, he became the best CI I have ever worked with. He never wanted any money. He graduated from high school and then took a job in a candy factory. Terrible backbreaking work, but it made him happy to contribute to his family. At first, he helped solve a number of robberies and burglaries that I was investigating and later provided crucial intelligence about some murders and drug deals..."

"Today, I was able to pick his brain for about 15 minutes before they got him. He said there did seem to be something unusual going on. He had heard that meetings had taken place between leaders of the Latin Kings and Latin Counts, who were normally bitter enemies. He didn't know what it was about, but rumors had also been going around that the Asian gangs were somehow involved in whatever it was. He had heard about the shootings in Chinatown but didn't think the Latin Kings were involved. For one, he said they wouldn't farm out the work to Asian shooters. They would do it themselves, and secondly, he said they don't do business in Chinatown, and the Asians don't come here. I don't know what it was about this kid Jack, but he touched my heart. I felt like the older sister he lost. He was so passionate about stopping the gangs from selling the drugs. Especially heroin. He had an idea that he had just told me about today..."

"He said the only way to stop it is to take the money away. Take away the money, and they wouldn't even be able to afford guns and wouldn't have to fight over drug turf. He wasn't sure how to do it, but he said it would be better to have clinics give the drugs away and offer treatment than give all the drug money to the gangs. It makes you think!"

"He also told me that he would gladly give his life to prevent thousands more Manuellas from dying because of this. And then, only seconds later, this punk road up on a red mountain bike and shot him in the head. He just stopped and looked right at me and grinned. I guess he could see that I wasn't wearing a gun. I wished that I had one more than any other time in my life. Then he just slowly rolled away, and I was left holding young Chico's head in my hands. I felt so sad and hopeless. But I am okay now. We have work to do. Thank you for listening, Jack."

"No problem, partner," I responded. "You know I've always got your back. Let's go figure this thing out." And soon, we pulled into the parking lot on N. Larrabee Street and got back to work.

When we walked in, all of the team members were there, including Marek and Chan. I first asked to see if Lieutenant Whitehead was available to sit in on the meeting but was told that he was called out to the scene of a homicide in River North. And so, the beat goes on.

Everyone sat down at their desks, and I asked Morgan Latner to lead off with a report on what he and Henrique Sanchez had been investigating. He began with the interview they had with Harry Sachman, the Head of Purchasing at Maxi-Mart. He described a well-dressed, sophisticated man of 51 years, who seemed surprisingly nervous and distracted. He portrayed the dinner party as being largely uneventful and cordial up until all hell broke loose. Once the bombs went off, he immediately left the premises and was driven away by his car service, which was waiting for him. He had seen the famous ancient artwork but said it was unremarkable to him but admitted art wasn't really his thing. He was invited to the party by Deputy Consulate General Li Yong. He was somewhat surprised to see one of his major competitors, Francine Vito from North American Imports, at the party when he arrived.

He then told us that the day after the party, he had been contacted by an assistant to Deputy General Fong Wu. He was told that there were some irregularities found with his company's purchasing practices and that he would be required to explain them or risk losing their status as an approved company. It caused him a great deal of concern. He had no idea what they were talking about, but he couldn't afford to lose the enormous number of products supplied to Maxi-Mart by Chinese manufacturers. Of course, he isn't worried about it anymore since less than two hours later, he was shot dead on N. Michigan Ave. "I'll get back to that later."

Morgan continued to describe a meeting with Sachman's competitor from North American Imports, Francine Vito, an attractive slender woman with dark hair and also in her early 50s.

Francine Vito was pleasant and totally in command. She described the dinner party along the same lines as Harry Sachman, and had gone straight home after exiting the townhouse. She was invited to the party by Deputy General Fong Wu and was also scheduled to meet with her later today. She said that business was good and that despite some tariff complications, they were back buying at pre-COVID levels. She reported no problems with supply chains or the consulates that she dealt with in Chicago or New Orleans.

After we supervised the crime scene at Sachman's murder, we had a chance to view some of the videos from several of the neighbors on N. Astor Street. The camera showed that all of the guests poured out of the townhouse along with the catering services and cooks initially. Everyone could be accounted for except the consulate officials. But very quickly after the first wave of action outside of the front door, the whole front of the townhouse was engulfed in smoke which obscured the view of the sidewalk front steps and door for about seven minutes. We don't know who may have come out or gone back into the house. No one coming out that we could see seemed to be carrying anything other than cell phones.

Next up, Detective Zilene Baker spoke for herself and Detective Kozlowski. She started with interviews of the two financial advisors, Harriot Bingham and Dominic Blasi. They interviewed investment banker Bingham at her office at Chicago First Multinational, early that morning. She presented as a very intelligent and confident businesswoman. She expressed that she and Chicago First Multinational had been trying to secure major Chinese clients looking to invest in various financial instruments or to borrow money for large-scale projects. She was invited to the dinner party by Deputy Consulate General Fong Wu and wasn't particularly bothered by the presence of a competitor such as Dominic Blasi since she didn't think he could compete with the resources of her bank.

Ms. Bingham said that the party was uneventful other than viewing their unusual ancient Chinese artifact and enjoying a great dinner. She didn't notice any problems, disagreements, or misunderstandings. Everything was fine until the smoke bombs went off. She then went straight to her car, parked nearby, and went home after stopping for a drink at Hugo's Frog Bar.

Detective Baker continued to say that they caught up with financial advisor Dominic Blasi at his suite of offices in the Monadnock Building on W. Jackson Blvd. His story was very similar to that of Bingham; except that he was invited to the party by Deputy General Li Qjang Yong. He also took exception with banker Bingham's claim that he couldn't compete with Chicago First Multinational. He said that he has a portfolio worth several billion dollars and represents hedge fund managers and private equity groups, capable of investing substantial amounts of money in Chinese projects.

78

The high-tech representatives at the party described their involvement with the dinner party along the same lines as the other guests. Li Zen, the Director of US operations for the Shanghai Power and Technology Company, presented as a powerfully built man of average height with short-cropped gray hair. He said that he was invited to the party by Fong Wu, and he has dealt with the Chinese Consulate of Chicago for years. He also stated that he doesn't know much about future Mindscape Industries or CEO Grace Tobin."

Their interview with Grace Tobin at her office at Future Mindscape revealed nothing new. She had dealt mainly with Deputy General Li Yong so far, but was scheduled to meet with Deputy General Fong Wu that afternoon.

I stood up after Zilene Baker sat down and told the team that this already complicated case had just gotten more so. I informed them about the identity of the young female server found dead on the top floor of the townhouse, and the likelihood that she was murdered by a massive hot shot that exploded her heart. We went over our visit to Pilsen and the cold-blooded murder of Elaina's CI at Benito Juarez Park.

The playing field had changed. It now seemed likely that various Chinese and Latino gangs may be involved. I relayed that we had made contact with two Lower Westside Gang Unit Detectives at the Canton Regio, just before the shooting in the park interrupted the meeting. We would follow up with them later.

I told the team to keep digging deeper into their people of interest and any connections they may have with Chinese or Latin criminal operations. I asked if anyone had any questions. The silence was only broken when Koz piped in. He stood up and said he was wondering how difficult it must have been for Agent Charlie Chan to eat tacos with chopsticks. Koz seemed really proud of himself after such a witty comment and looked around the room with a stupid shit-eating grin on his fat face.

No one seemed to be amused, and I was furious and tried hard to keep it under wraps. I looked fiercely at Kozlowski, which caused him to lose the silly grin, and said, "I wouldn't know about that, Koz, but I think we are all wondering how difficult it is for you to talk without a brain. Now sit down and try to think about that."

Kozlowski sheepishly sat down and seemed confounded about what I had just said. I figured that was as good it was going to get with him. I ended the meeting and left it open about the next time we needed to meet, but asked everyone to keep in touch with me. I would coordinate with Whitehead.

I looked at Elaina and said, "I think we all need a beer." Chan and Marek said they were in, so we headed out to Timothy O'Toole's.

When we arrived, the place was hopping, so we started toward the only available booth just as three people finished up at the bar leaving four open seats. We hustled over and sat down, ready to order. A bartender named DJ came right over and said hello and, after some quick introductions, took our orders of Millers for Henry and me and Coronas for Elaina and Teresa. I was about to order shots of Jack Daniels, but Elaina beat me to it and ordered four Herradura tequilas. I was absolutely up for it, but Henry and Teresa declined. DJ asked how we wanted them, and Elaina wanted lemon and no salt. I nodded in approval.

The beers came first, and we clinked bottles and said, "Here's to never a dull moment." It was one of my mom's favorite sayings and always made me smile no matter the situation. We all took a long deep drink and sat back in quietude.

Feeling a little more relaxed, I noticed a familiar presence behind me and heard an even more familiar voice say, "Mom used to save that one for special occasions. What's going on, Jackie?"

I immediately knew who it was without looking back. It was my older brother Barry one of O'Toole's managers. He already knew Elaina, so I introduced him to Teresa and Henry. After a brief exchange of the most recent events in our lives, he continued managing a nearly full house on this early summer evening. I thought it would be wise to exchange a few ideas before we got too far into the beers and tequilas. But first, the Herraduras arrived, and DJ decided to join us. Elaina led the toast, and we touched glasses to salute her lost friend Chico, and put them down topped off with a taste of lemon.

It was time to refocus, and we exchanged ideas for a while. Agents Chan and Marek were able to put the global heroin picture in perspective for us. Henry didn't see some kind of marriage between the Latino and Asian factions as making any sense in Chicago. He didn't think that the Latin gangs needed any help from Chinatown or Argyle Street for either supply or distribution of any type of drugs in the city or suburbs.

Teresa noted that most of the heroin coming to Chicago began with poppies grown in the Asian triangle of Afghanistan, Pakistan and Northern India. It gets shipped to Mexico, refined and then transported to Chicago and other parts of the US across the border in trucks, cars, planes and boats. It is then brought up in various ways. Much of it entering Chicago by truck and car, eventually ending up on the Eisenhower Expressway, often referred to in law enforcement circles as the Heroin Highway.

The Chinese gangs had been minor players at best, and there simply wasn't a large population of Asian heroin users in Chicago. Even though there seemed to be strong indications that something was going on, nobody had any idea what it was.

I felt that we needed to focus on what we did know and go from there—starting with the events of Saturday night.

"We have two murder victims who don't seem to have any relationship. Is there a connection? And if so, what? Also, at the same time, a priceless artifact is stolen. Does that have any relation to either of the murders and if so, what?"

"We also have an attempted murder on one of the other top officials from the Chinese Consulate leaving the other Deputy Counsel General as either a suspect or the next target. Then we have an assassination attempt on a dinner guest who is a local businesswoman from Chinatown and now this morning a successful hit on one of the most influential businessmen in the country. What in hell is the connection here? There has to be something. We need to keep digging. We need to keep looking at every angle. We will figure this fucking thing out, people."

I raised my beer glass, and the others followed. We ordered more beers and enjoyed talking about anything and everything for a while. It was good to see Elaina smile a little. We had some fun kidding each other about our favorite baseball teams, with Elaina and Henry bragging about the White Sox and Teresa and I promising a resurgence for the Cubs. Turns out that Teresa's father grew up in Kenosha, where I now have learned that there are a lot of Cub fans. Who knew?

Before it got too late, Henry and Teresa said their good nights and promised to see us in the morning. Elaina and I ordered one more beer had a chance to talk about what had happened in Pilsen just hours before. Mainly I sat and listened. It seemed to be cathartic for my partner and even made me feel better about what she went through at the park.

As we finished our beers, I told her I needed to ask her something. She said, "Sure, Jack, go-ahead."

"I have to say that those Gang Detectives Santos and Bulger were pretty intimidating guys."

She just laughed and kept looking at me as if to say, and so what's the question? I was searching for the question. "Elaina, I have to say that I was surprised to see the way Santos reacted and got down and comforted you in the park."

"Oh, that!" she said, laughing again. "You see I have known José most of my life. He grew up with my older brother Javy. He was always at our house. He was practically part of our family. He used to call me 'mi hermanita.' His little sister. But you are not wrong. I feel sorry for that little punk if Jose and Devin find him first. That's all I'm going to say about that.

Elaina insisted on taking the check, and we walked out of the cool downstairs bar into a particularly steamy Chicago summer night. We told each other to take care and were off on our separate ways.

I got into my Camaro and took Ontario Street to Michigan Ave., heading north and stayed on when it merged with Lakeshore Drive. I usually enjoyed the ride home along the Lake, but my mind was racing. So much had happened during the last few days that it was impossible to slow the process down.

I kept the top and the windows down even though the heat was nearly stifling. I needed to feel the air on my face. It didn't really help much. When I got to my exit, I turned East toward Lake Michigan instead of the usual left to my apartment. I felt compelled to go to the water. As I pulled into the parking lot for Montrose Beach, I noticed a couple of cars still there but didn't see or hear anyone around. I knew what I was going to do. I left my coat and wallet in the car and made sure they were locked up, and my Beretta and Star were double-locked into the glove compartment before hitting the sand. Again, I didn't see anyone, so I found a spot about 10 feet from the water and quickly lost my clothes. I sprinted directly into the Lake and ran, galloping through the shallow until it was up to my waist, and then dove in.

The coolness of the water was just what I needed. I swam out and kept swimming until I started breathing hard and losing steam. My near exhaustion was somehow comforting. It cleared my mind.

83

I stopped and began treading, not bothering to look back to the shore to see how far out I was. The pitch black of that overcast evening was mesmerizing. The silent nothingness was so appealing. I felt like I was being beckoned into a realm of calm and peace. So, I went with it and kept treading water and looking out into the intoxicating blackness.

But then I felt a change. It was subtle at first. A slight breeze from the north. A tiny ripple on the surface. The breeze then became a wind. The ripples became small waves. The spell was broken. I turned around to see that I was several hundred yards from the shore. Somehow my colossal tumultuous city was calling me back. I could almost hear it saying to me, "You're not going anywhere. I am not done with you yet. This is where you belong. Come home to me."

Chapter 9

I woke up on Tuesday morning after a deep, much-needed sleep. No alarm was set, and I didn't worry about how long I slept. I made it to around eight and woke up to mostly clear skies with a stiff breeze coming through my open windows. The weather had changed dramatically overnight. The oppressive heat had broken and was replaced by cooler, dryer air. My kind of day.

My morning shower felt great, and my bowl of frosted flakes tasted even better than usual. I seemed to be reenergized and optimistic. I texted Elaina to let her know that I would be coming into the station a little late, and she responded that she was also running late due to her helping Chico's family with the arrangements for his funeral. I told her to take her time and offered to help if she needed me. She said thanks and would let me know. Before hanging up with her, I told her that I would check in with Lieutenant Whitehead and hopefully get some good news about our reinstatement to full duty.

So, I finished my morning routine and hit the road. This time the breeze through the open windows in the Camaro felt refreshing and motivating. My crazy case seemed less daunting and more like a welcome challenge.

After parking in the lot, I walked into the building smiling. Immediately, I sensed that people noticed. I realized that police officers and detectives don't usually walk around smiling and looking happy. It wasn't normal for me either. But at that moment, I didn't care. I just wanted to feel that way for a while.

Inside the detective's room's Zilene Baker looked up and smiled back at me. Kozlowski glanced toward me, snarled, and looked back at his computer. Morgan Latner shot me a *what's up with you* look. He had seen me happy before but not at work, and

Henrique chuckled to himself and said something in Spanish. I was fine with not understanding what he said.

Lieutenant Whitehead popped his head into the room and said, "Fallon in my office right now." His tone of voice and obviously serious nature took the smile off my face and the edge off my mood. *Okay,* I thought, *it was back to reality.*

When I walked into his office, he told me to close the door and sit down in a firm but calm manner. There was no small talk with Whitehead. He got directly to the point. "Jack, I had a long conversation with Senior Special Agent William Manion this morning. He has been supervising Agents Chan and Marek and is primarily responsible for the high level of cooperation from the FBI on our investigation. He has a great deal of pressure from Washington to have the body of Consulate General Zhao Chen released to the consulate. And, since we have performed a complete autopsy, we will return the favor to the FBI and let the consulate have the body. Also, you and Rodriguez will no longer be allowed to operate under FBI supervision. However, I have been able to have internal affairs expedite their decision on the shooting in Chinatown. They have reinstated you and Detective Rodriguez to full active duty and released your weapons on a temporary basis until they officially complete the investigation."

Senior Special Agent Manion also told me about their undercover Agent Kira Vu Sing, our second victim at N. Astor Street., and the reason she was placed in that situation. I understand that you and Rodriguez, with Chan and Marek, have been working on the heroin angle as part of your investigation. I want you to keep going with that. Follow it wherever it leads. I know things are moving fast and that the killing of Elaina's CI in Pilsen hit her hard. She can have some time this morning, but I need you two back on the case with everything you've got. Make good use of your full duty status. I don't want to think that I stuck my neck out getting you reinstated for nothing."

"Got it, Lieutenant." I said enthusiastically as I stood up. We are all in..."

"You had better be..." were his words that followed me out of his office along with, "You and Rodriguez can sign out your weapons at the front desk."

I returned to the detective's room and checked in with Elaina. She said that she was on her way and ready to get to work. She sounded like herself. It was good to hear.

Baker and Kozlowski were headed out to follow up on their interviews from Monday, and Latner and Sanchez were already doing the same. Agents Marek and Chan messaged me that they were headed my way, and I figured they would arrive about the same time as Elaina. The timing was perfect since the desk Sgt. had just walked into the room with a message from Deputy Consulate General Fong Wu. She wanted to see us at the consulate in an hour.

As soon as Elaina arrived, I told her about my meeting with Whitehead, and we went together to the front desk and signed for our guns. It felt good to be fully back in action. We knew that the shootings in Chinatown were justified and were not worried about the final outcome of the Internal Affairs investigation.

Agents Chan and Marek appeared shortly thereafter, and we huddled for a few minutes exchanging information and any new developments with the agents in Quantico, Virginia. It was determined that at least one of the three dead shooters from Sunday night at The East Asian Sounds club, was a known gun for hire from Shanghai named Wey Lao. They were trying to determine if the other two were known associates of Lao.

As far as the stolen artwork went, they couldn't detect any indication that it was being shopped through legitimate dealers or offered on the Internet or any deep web network they were monitoring. It seemed that whoever had it was either being very patient or was simply content to keep it for themselves.

I invited our FBI partners to accompany us to see Fong Wu at the Chinese Consulate, and they eagerly accepted. I figured it would be good to have their experience and expertise to help evaluate the mysterious Deputy General.

We decided to drive together, so we all got into our Impala, and Elaina resumed her usual position as driver, with Marek and Chan taking the backseat. As we were pulling up in front of 1 E. Erie Street, we noticed two uniform Chinese military personnel stationed outside the front door. The shot-out windows on the first floor had been replaced, but a heightened sense of security came with them. Inside, two more uniformed guards were looking very unhappy to see us.

As the guards approached us menacingly, we braced for a possible confrontation. When we neared the elevators, one of them opened, and a large commanding figure emerged. It was the familiar unpleasant person of Yi Peng, consulate official and seemingly an assistant to Deputy General Fong Wu. He barked orders in Chinese to the guards, who stepped quickly back and looked like they wanted to disappear. He then turned his piercing gaze toward us, and only a slightly less intimidating voice informed us that Deputy Wu was waiting for us. We were to follow him. So, after a slight hesitation, we did.

The elevator ride up to their offices was a silent affair. We followed "Lurch" out into the fifth-floor hallway, where two more uniformed guards were stationed outside the entrance. A slight motion of Yi Peng's right-hand caused the guards to move quickly away from the doorway, and we followed this hulk of a man as he fairly burst through the doors into the consulate.

Instantaneously, Fong Wu's other assistant, Hu Ying, the spry graceful woman with a sense of calm and aplomb that seemed exaggerated compared to Yi Peng, appeared and approached us. She greeted us pleasantly by name and informed us that the Deputy General was expecting us. She asked us to follow her, and as we did, I looked around and noticed that our buddy Lurch had disappeared.

We were greeted at the door of the spacious corner office by Deputy Consulate General Fong Wu. She invited us to sit down in four chairs arranged precisely for our meeting. She placed me next to her with Elaina, Henry and Teresa in that order. She was meticulous and liked to be in control. The energy and ambition that she exuded answered the unasked question of how she had risen to such a lofty diplomatic position customarily reserved for men in China. I had to wonder if that had made her a target.

When we were all seated, she remained standing at first as she spoke to us. Another control technique, I thought. She didn't miss a trick. "Thank you all for coming. I am sorry that I wasn't available to meet with you sooner, but the events of the last few days have been very unsettling. Very unfortunate. The loss of our Consulate General Zhao Chen has been a heavy blow to the consulate and to me personally. He was a mentor to me. He knew my family in Beijing where he worked closely in the Party with my father and was kind enough to take me under his wing when I showed interest in the Diplomatic Service."

With that, she sat down behind her sleek modern steel and glass desk, which was completely absent of any clutter. Actually, it was absent of anything other than a phone and a computer.

I felt that I needed to break through her presentation and take a little control myself. "I understand how difficult these last few days have been for you and the entire Trade Office," I said. "But may I ask you some questions, Deputy Wu?"

She nodded and smiled as if to say, *you may ask, but I am still in control.*

"I would like to begin with the dinner party Saturday night on N. Astor Street." Deputy Wu smiled, nodding, and I continued.

"Tell me how the idea for the gathering that included a private showing of the Egg of Chaos came about."

The Deputy General seemed to have anticipated the question. "Consulate General Chen had been wanting to do a series of these small dinners that would include some prominent people that either were doing substantial business with China, or who wished to do so. He was very knowledgeable about Chinese history and philosophies and especially the idea of balancing the forces of the universe. The Yin Yang. It was his idea to invite some leading people in several different industries. He felt that the competition would produce a beneficial outcome. And when it was announced that there would be an exhibit of Han Dynasty artifacts coming to the Art Institute, he had the idea to invite the two art historians and to have a private showing of one of the artworks. When the Egg of Chaos was made available, he couldn't have been more pleased."

"Who chose the people that would be invited?" I asked.

"The Consulate General decided to have each of his Deputies choose one from the different industries. I think he also liked the idea of competition between his deputies." she said with that smile.

"Do you think that competition had anything to do with the Consul General's murder and the attempt on your life?" I inquired. This time the smile left her face, and her eyes flashed an intensity I had not seen before.

"I sincerely hope not." she answered. "I would never suspect Deputy General, Qjang or anyone else from here, she said firmly. I am not trying to say that I think any of the guests would do this either, but I don't know. All of the hostile talk that has been directed at China here could cause some unfortunate animosity. So, of course, we want you to solve this mystery. That is why I am choosing to speak to you detectives."

"We appreciate that." I said. "Which of the guests did you choose?"

She responded that she had chosen an investment banker Harriet Bingham, importer, Francine Vito technology industrialist, Li Zen, and Professor Nils Borland. She picked them mainly because she had met them at various functions in the past. She also had invited businessman Herbert Long from Little Saigon, whom she had been acquainted with for several years.

Deputy Consulate General Li Qjang had chosen financial consultant Dominic Blasi, Harry Sackman from Maxi-Mart, technology developer Grace Tobin, Chinatown businesswoman Lily Mai Tong and Art Curator Belinda Carlisle."

"Were you familiar with any of those guests?" I asked.

"Only Harry Sackman." She answered. "Maxi-Mart is one of the biggest buyers of Chinese products in the world. He was well-known here and at the Chinese Embassy in Washington. His death was very shocking."

Do you know whether Deputy General Qjang knew any of the guests prior to the dinner party?"

"He definitely knew Mr. Sackman and Li Zen from Shanghai Power and Technology, and he met the Art Curator before the dinner to make final arrangements for the Egg of Chaos. The others, I do not think so."

"You mentioned your long-standing relationship with Consulate General Chen. But did you know Deputy General, Qjang before you started working here in Chicago? "

She explained that she had heard of him but had never met him. He was from Shanghai, and their paths had never crossed.

"What is your relationship with him like?" I continued.

She hesitated before answering for the first time. Her voice lowered, and she seemed a little troubled by the question. "We are from different regions, and even though he isn't that much older, he seems to be from another generation. We have different views of the world. He is very old-fashioned, very conservative. I think we should become more involved with the local community. He prefers to keep a distance."

"I don't want to suggest anything, but who is in charge of the consulate now?" I asked.

She shook her head a little and answered, "We both have an equal say right now. We have not been informed of anything by Beijing."

"Have either of you formally requested to have the top job?" I wanted to know.

She laughed a little." No, we don't need to do that. It is assumed that we both want to be Consulate General."

"I have just one more question. What position does that big fellow Yi Peng have here? He seems to be a bit hyper-serious, if you know what I mean."

Her smile returned. "He should be." she said. "He is the Head of Consulate Security."

"Who chose him for the job?" I asked.

"I am not sure," she replied. "He was already here when I started. I am the junior deputy. All of the primary staff were already here."

"By the way, where is he from?"

"He is from Shanghai," she responded.

"May I ask where he was on Saturday night? No one saw him at the N. Astor Street party."

"Oh, he was there. It is his business at times to be somewhat invisible. He has his ways. He is very good at his job. Sometimes very mysterious, I think."

"Thank you very much for your time, Deputy General Wu. We appreciate your help and cooperation."

"You are very welcome," she said as we all stood up.

"One more thing," I said. "We would like to follow up with Deputy General Qjang. Is he available?"

"I am afraid not: Fong Wu answered. "He is making the arrangements to have Consulate General Zhao Chen's body returned to his family in Beijing. We are both very grateful to your Department Detectives Fallon and Rodriguez and, of course, to FBI Agents Chan and Marek. I will walk you out and send you on your way."

And so away we went.

Chapter 10

When we got to the car, we had a quick discussion about what had just transpired at the consulate. The FBI agents agreed that it was unusual for a Chinese official with diplomatic immunity to allow herself to be interviewed by FBI agents or local police in any kind of a criminal investigation. They had done their homework on the Chicago consulate officials. They confirmed that what Deputy Wu had said about her background and relationship with former Consulate General Chen was verified by their sources at the CIA. While Wu's family was prominent in the Communist Party, some had been wildly successful in the banking and technology industries. One of her sisters was one of China's first female self-made billionaires, having created an extensive network of financial institutions.

The information they had on Deputy Consulate General Li Qjang also matched what she had told them. He was from the Shanghai region. His family is similarly involved in Communist Party politics and had been moderately successful in the shipping industry, which wasn't unusual since the Yang Shon Port of Shanghai is the busiest in the world.

None of us were sure whether there was any significance in which Deputy General had invited which dinner guests, but we all thought it was worth looking into further. We decided to start by talking to Herbert Long, the businessman from Chinatown Northside. Agent Chan had a couple of phone numbers for businessman Herbert Long and was able to get in touch with him and arranged to meet with him in about an hour at one of his restaurants on Argyle Street.

Before leaving for the Sun, Ky BBQ, I decided to check in with our detective partners. Detectives Baker and Kozlowski were in the process of reinterviewing the two high-tech moguls, Li Zen and

Grace Tobin. They had just left the offices of Shanghai Power and Technology and were on their way to see Grace Tobin at Future Mindscape Industries on the Near Southside. Detective Baker reported that they had not learned much new from Li Zen other than he has known Deputy Consul General Li Qjang Yong for many years going back to his early days starting out in business in Shanghai.

Next, I got in touch with Detective Latner. He and Detective Sanchez had already reinterviewed Francine Vito from North American imports. She expressed a deep feeling of sadness about the murder of Harry Sachman, Head of Purchasing for Maxi-Mart. Ms. Vito was unaware of any serious threat to Mr. Sachman other than the many threatening letters and emails that they both receive from people expressing anger over their extensive business dealings with China. She claimed that she didn't consider Harry Sachman to be a competitor as much as she thought of him to be a colleague.

After that, we headed north to Little Saigon. Elaina chose to go by way of the Lakeshore Drive, and we all enjoyed the ride on this picture-perfect summer afternoon. With the windows down, the dry, warm air wafted throughout the car and brought a smile to my face as we rushed along the lake, gazing out on the boats in the water and hikers, runners, and bike riders on the lake path.

Before long, we exited Lakeshore Drive in my neighborhood of Uptown and made our way up Broadway to Argyle Street and the Sun, Ky BBQ Chinese and Vietnamese restaurant owned by Herbert long.

When we arrived, we were greeted outside by a young Asian woman who directed us to one of the sidewalk tables and told us that Mr. Long would join us shortly. She took our order for some iced teas and soft drinks, and just as they arrived, so did Herbert Long. He introduced himself all around and took a seat with us. He invited us to order whatever we wanted from the menu, but we decided to concentrate on the interview. I asked him about how he came to be invited to the dinner party on N. Astor Street, and he confirmed that he had met Deputy General Fong Wu a couple of times at various social functions previously but otherwise didn't know the other dinner guests except Lily Mai Tong. He said that everyone in Chicago's Asian community knew of her as one of the wealthiest and most influential business leaders in Chinatown. He also made sure to explain that they were not direct competitors.

I asked him about the general relationship that the gangs from Chinatown and Little Saigon had. He responded that it was generally good, although there has been a history of rivalry between the On Leong Tong in Chinatown and the Hip Sing Tong of Argyle Street. He said that the tongs or gangs are now essentially political organizations, and their members are older, more mature adults, unlike the younger street gangs.

I wanted to know if he had noticed any unusual gang-related or other activities in Little Saigon. He said there was nothing that he was aware of, but he didn't know everything that went on in the neighborhood. Specifically, I wanted to know whether he knew of any possible interaction between the Asian street gangs in Little Saigon or even Chinatown with Latin street gangs. Again, he said that that he didn't know of any.

Just then, his phone chimed, and he answered it without leaving the table. He engaged in a brief conversation in Chinese. I had no idea what was being said, but while he was talking, I noticed agent Marek's eyes light up. He ended the conversation and apologized for the interruption.

I decided to go in a different direction with my questions and asked him where he grew up. He smiled and answered that he had mostly grown up right here in the Uptown neighborhood after moving with his family from China to Chicago when he was nine years old.

"I couldn't help noticing that you seem to speak Chinese fluently. I don't understand any of it, but it is still impressive to me. Was that Mandarin you were speaking?" I inquired further. He nodded and said that his family spoke Mandarin at home, and he grew up speaking English as a second language.

"You certainly seem to speak English very well now." I said.

Herbert Long smiled again and said, "Thank you. Yes. It is now very good, but I had to work very hard at it."

This time it was my phone that buzzed, and it was an excited Zilene Baker on the other end. "Jack, we just got to Future Mindscape, and all hell broke loose! When we pulled into the parking lot, we heard muffled gunshots and saw two men running away from a black Mercedes, which was running with the driver's side door open and the limp body of a middle-aged woman hanging out. We jumped out, drew our weapons, and ordered the two men to stop. They fucking stopped, but they turned and started firing on us. Koz was hit twice and is down. The EMTs just got here and are taking him to the hospital. They are also transporting the woman from the black Mercedes. It turned out to be our person of interest Grace Tobin. What in the hell do we have going on here, Jack?"

"I wish I fucking knew!" I exclaimed. "We will be right there."

We all rushed into our Impala, and as soon as the doors shut, Agent Teresa Marek fairly erupted with revelations about what she had heard during their meeting with Herbert Long. "That guy is dirty as hell!" She blurted out. "We know that he is lying about not having any knowledge about any contacts in the Little Saigon with the Latinos. Hell, we know he did himself. He's up to his ass in all this, whatever the hell this is."

"Teresa, did you get anything from the phone call he took?" I asked.

"Sure did." she responded. "First of all, the call just confirmed another lie, as I suspected after hearing a little of his conversation with the Security Chief from the Consulate the last time we were there. He says that he is from the North of China and speaks Mandarin, but he clearly speaks with the Wu dialect from Shanghai. And I can't be sure, but I think he was talking on the phone to the same guy, Yi Peng. It was definitely also someone speaking Shanghainese. They were talking about an important event happening tonight and confirmed that they had reservations this evening for the sunset dinner cruise from Navy pier. I sure as hell would like to know what that was all about."

"Me too!" I exclaimed. "What do you think, Elaina?" She looked at me as if to say, *what are you waiting for?* I turned to Henry and Teresa and saw that they obviously agreed. "We are in!" Chan offered.

As we continued our short drive to Future Mindscape Industries, I got online and reserved a table for four on the cruise ship Odyssey for the three-hour dinner cruise leaving from Navy pier at 7 PM.

When we got within a block of the scene, we could see flashing blue and red lights and hear the sirens as the ambulances raced away.

At the sprawling complex, the large parking lot was full of marked and unmarked police cars. We parked as close as we could to what appeared to be the heart of the crime scene and got out. The warm afternoon air still smelled like gunpowder, and light ribbons of smoke still drifted in the breeze.

I quickly noticed Detective Zilene Baker was talking to a couple of other detectives. I recognized one of them as Mary Zorn but not the other guy. They weren't from the Near North but were probably called in because of the police shooting. I asked Elaina and the agents to spread out and see what they could learn. Then I waited to talk to Detective Baker. Eventually, Zilene wrapped up her conversation with the detectives. Detective Zorn confiscated her 9 mm Glock, and they parted ways. Detective Zorn nodded to me as I approached and got into the driver's side of their sedan.

I treaded lightly toward Zilene and could see the troubled look on her face. I have known her for nearly three years and had always thought she was one of the smartest and strongest detectives I had known in Chicago. I got to her and just stood there without words. I stood looking into her eyes and imagining powerful feelings of anger and guilt.

Finally, I broke the silence. "Zilene, how is Koz doing?"

She hesitated and looked directly at me with her strong dark eyes. "He's not good, Jack. He got hit in the stomach and the shoulder. The EMTs responded as fast as they could, but he lost a lot of blood."

"What the hell happened, Zilene?" She responded that they were pulling up for a scheduled interview with Grace Tobin and could see her drive into the parking lot at the same time. She parked in a reserved spot near the entrance, and we took a spot a little further away.

"As we began getting out, two guys zoomed up to Tobin's car on motorcycles and pulled out pistols and shot her before she even got out of her car. Koz was in the passenger seat closer to Tobin's car and jumped out ahead of me. He ran right toward the two guys dressed in black, yelling for them to drop their weapons and identifying us as Chicago PD. They turned on him and didn't hesitate to shoot him. He didn't get off a shot. I think he held up because Grace Tobin was in his line of fire. I got off a few shots as they drove away, but I don't think that I hit them."

"Did you get a good look at the shooters?" I wanted to know.

"Not really," she answered. "They were totally covered up in black clothes and wore helmets with tinted visors. They were short, slender, and seemed young. They looked to be very agile on the bikes and definitely knew how to handle them."

After a while, Elaina and the agents joined us and expressed condolences and best wishes about Koz. Elaina reported that Grace Tobin's injuries were also severe, and she was being taken to the University of Illinois Hospital on W. Taylor Street. Agent Chan found a couple of witnesses who verified Zilene's account of the shooting and the general description of the shooters. They described the motorcycles as being sleek and unusually quiet and were either blue or purple. Agent Marek said that shell casings were found near Grace Tobin's car and looked to be 350 caliber. They also found some 9 mm casings near where Zilene took a few shots at the perpetrators.

Then my phone buzzed, and it was Lieut. Whitehead. His voice sounded deeper and even more serious than usual. He had heard about the shootings and was aware that Detective Kozlowski was on his way to Stroger Hospital. "Jack, this fucking thing is spiraling out of control. We have to get a handle on it, and I mean now!" He bellowed with a rising volume that somehow seemed more like a roar than a statement.

I filled him in on what we knew about what had just happened in the parking lot, the evidence found, and the witness statements, including that of Detective Baker. I then described her meeting with Herbert Long on Argyle Street and what Teresa Marek overheard. Whitehead liked my idea of following whatever was going on with the dinner cruise and wanted to be kept informed.

As I finish the conversation with Lieut. Whitehead Detectives Morgan Latner and Henrique Sanchez drove up. They had heard about the shooting and wanted to check in on their teammates. They were quickly brought up to speed and told of the plan to attend the dinner cruise from Navy pier. I told Morgan to stand by and that I would call him after going to Stroger to check on Koz.

Agents Marek and Chan wanted to report to their office before meeting us at Navy Pier at 6 PM. I planned to arrange to be let in on the ship early and be placed at a table in the back and away from Herbert Long and whoever he was meeting.

Elaina and I drove them back to the station on N. Larrabee Street to pick up their car. We then headed over to Stroger Hospital on W. Ogden Street. Once there, we entered the bustling hospital and were informed that Detective Kozlowski had gone directly from the emergency room to surgery. He was expected to be in surgery for quite a while.

We were directed to the waiting area, and there we joined Detective Baker sitting with Koz's wife, Anna, who looked like all of the blood had drained from her face. She seemed to be in shock, and Zilene was speaking softly and stroking her back. I had met Anna a couple of times but didn't really know her. Elaina and I sat down quietly and waited for news about our teammate.

About 1/2 hour later, a nurse came out to us and let us know that surgery was still underway but that Koz's vital signs were stable and the prognosis was good for him to make it through. The injuries were extremely serious, but they were hopeful for a full recovery.

Zilene said that she would stay at the hospital with Anna at least until he was out of surgery. I told her to do whatever she needed to and that I would be in touch later. Elaina and I said our goodbyes to Anna and wished her all the best. She thanked us and shook our hands warmly.

We had about 2 1/2 hours before meeting Marek and Chan at Navy Pier, and Elaina wanted to go back to Pilsen to see how Chico's family was doing with planning for the funeral. She had already raised nearly enough money for the wake and burial with the help of donations from many police officers from our district and Pilsen. She also had made plans for a mass at her parish church Saint Procopius for Friday.

I touched base with Morgan Latner, and we decided to meet at Doc B's Fresh Kitchen on Grand Avenue for a late lunch and to discuss this crazy case. Elaina took her Jeep down to Pilsen, and I kept the Impala since I was still on the job and would be well into the evening.

Morgan and Henrique were already at Doc B's when I arrived. I sat down at their table and ordered a root beer and some teriyaki chicken wings with their hand-battered fries and Cajun dipping sauce. Morgan chose the full rack of Danish ribs with coleslaw, and Henrique decided on the chimichurri steak with fries.

We devoured our food while exchanging ideas on the case interspersed with some suggestions on how to improve the Cubs pitching staff and the Bear special-teams.

Morgan believed there was a connection between the Chinese Consulate and the Chinese gangs in both the North and South sides, and Henrique thought the problem was between the Latino gangs and the Chinese Street gangs over drug turf.

We finished our lunch and put the finishing touches on a plan for that night. We agreed to see each other later and decided that the Cubs needed another starting pitcher and two relievers. None of us were sure about how to fix the Bear's special teams, so that was left for another day.

Chapter 11

I got to Navy Pier early and had plenty of time to take a stroll around the iconic Chicago landmark and attraction. Walking into the Pier's outside promenade, I passed Harry Caray's Pier location, various food court vendors, the famous Ferris Wheel, and several tour boats docked and being refreshed for their next excursion. About halfway down the length of the heavily populated Pier, I found the ship Odyssey.

It was too early for a line to have formed with passengers waiting to board. There were no crew members outside, so I slipped past the restraining rope and walked up the gangplank and up to the entrance to the dining room. As I entered, a uniformed crew member approached me. His demeanor, spotless Naval style white outfit and hat indicated a man of authority.

He introduced himself as Captain Moriarity, and I showed him my star, which I now was carrying in my pocket and my ID. I explained why I was arriving so early, and he responded that he had been notified and was expecting us. I confirmed that there would be four of us and that we were on the job and would be armed. I showed him that I was wearing a shoulder strap holster and Beretta. I rarely used the shoulder holster, but I didn't want it visible on my belt. We took a look at the registration list and found mine. We then looked for a familiar name, and sure enough, there was Herbert Long's table for six. He switched the table assignments so that we were in the furthest table back next to Windows and on the other side of the ship from Herbert Long, who was now assigned to the first table in the front.

I thanked Capt. Moriarity and said that I would be back with my party at six to get on well ahead of the other guests. The Captain said that would be fine and reminded me to pick up our tickets at the booth, which was about 30 feet away on the Pier. Walking down the gangplank, I saw the ticket booth and went over to get our four boarding passes. I couldn't help wondering whether I would be able to put a voucher in for this expensive trip. I hoped that at least the food would be good.

I made my way over to the food court, which was our designated meeting place. I ordered a Coke from McDonald's and sat at one of the only free tables among a bustling crowd of families and young tourists out on the day at Navy Pier. There was something very pleasing about the energy of the people on vacation, and in some cases, seeing Chicago and the Pier for the first time. I especially enjoyed watching the kids' excitement and wonderment of being in such a picturesque setting.

So, after spending about 1/2 an hour being entertained by the comings and goings at the food court, I was joined by Agents Marek and Chan and soon thereafter, my partner Elaina Rodriguez. I quickly filled them in on the game plan and handed out the boarding passes. It was almost six and time to board the Odyssey.

We took the short walk to the ship, and I was happy to see the Captain waiting for us at the gangplank. Introductions were made, and Capt. Moriarity personally showed us to our table in the back of the dining room and on the right side of the bar tucked into the corner. It was the most discrete spot in the room, and we figured it was the best we could do.

I decided it was best for Elaina and me to sit with our backs to the main dining area and let Henry Chan and Teresa Marek face into the room. She figured that since I had done most of the talking when interviewing Herbert Long and officials from the consulate, they were more likely to recognize me than the FBI agents. I wasn't sure who would show up, but that was my best bet.

We had some time before passengers would begin boarding, which allowed us to compare notes and catch up a little on this constantly changing case. Henry Chan started the conversation by letting us know that they were given some recently developed intelligence indicating that after years of declining poppy harvesting in China, there seems to be a significant uptick in production in several regions in the South. The information was new and sketchy but believed to come from reliable sources.

Teresa Marek added that this would be a fundamental change in Chinese government policy. They had stringent drug laws and sentencing, including the death penalty. However, there have been some significant changes happening in China, with many private individuals amassing huge fortunes, including a majority of the world's new women billionaires. And Deputy Consul General, Fong Wu's sister, was among them. On the other hand, Deputy Consulate General Li Qjang Yong's family was far from wealthy, having worked at the lower levels of the shipping industry in Shanghai.

I noticed that Elaina had been unusually quiet. She said that everything was okay, but it wasn't convincing. Before I could inquire any further, her phone lit up, and she answered it. Her facial expression was serious and intense. All I could hear was pretty vague, and it ended with her saying, "Okay, see you tomorrow."

Elaina didn't offer any information about the phone call but did share that she had spent the afternoon helping Chico's family with arrangements for his funeral set for Friday morning. They had already begun the 48-hour wake, which would continue the next day leading up to the funeral mass and burial on Friday.

Just then, the Captain stopped by our table and asked us if we would like to tour the ship before the passengers were allowed on board. I quickly accepted his invitation, and we started at our end of the dining room. The bar was directly to our right and was a little bit in front of us, giving us some privacy. On the other side of the bar was a narrow hallway from which guests could take an immediate right turn to the bathrooms or walk a little further and walked up a flight of stairs to the upper deck of the ship, that was laid out with some couches and tables which still left a lot of open space in the center and at the railings. The air was warm and breezy. It was a perfect day for this kind of venture out on Lake Michigan, to enjoy the spectacular view of Chicago's magnificent skyline.

Capt. Moriarity explained that the passengers would start boarding in about 10 minutes at 6:30, and the ship would be ready to leave the pier at about 7:15. Dinner orders would be taken right away, and everyone would be served no later than 8:00 or 8:15. There was a dessert station and a small dance floor that sometimes saw a lot of action.

We all wandered around the upper deck for a few minutes looking over the layout. I noticed that we were somewhere around 30 feet up and thought that even a fall into the Lake would possibly be hazardous and that a jump onto the promenade would be perilous.

I asked the Captain how crowded it got up there, and he responded that most people would at least come up to check it out, and on a nice day, some spend most of the trip there. He also added that on Wednesdays and Saturdays, Navy Pier had fireworks show which drew a bigger crowd than usual.

Moriarty led us back down the stairs and on a walk through the dining room, which had aisles on each side running along the tables set at the windows, and tables across from them in the interior of the room. At the end of the dining room, a doorway led to a small outer deck with only a couple of stand-up tables and no chairs or couches. This deck was approximately 15 feet up.

We walked back through the dining room and took our seats. I wasn't sure what to expect from Herbert Long's dinner party or even who would be there. It could simply be a night out with legitimate business partners or family and friends, but I felt that we needed to check it out. It was our best lead at the moment.

The passengers began filing in and were guided to their assigned tables. The servers started taking drink and dinner orders right away. We all chose salads, and Elaina and I chose the braised short ribs and the FBI agents both took the salmon.

Our table was the first to order, so our iced teas and coffees were being delivered when Teresa Marek spotted Herbert Long walk in, accompanied by my buddy Lurch. It was Yi Peng, Head of Security at the Chinese Consulate. They were soon followed by Francine Vito from North American Importers, Li Zen from Shanghai Power and Technologies and financiers, Harriet Bingham and Dominic Blasi. Their positioning was perfect at the first table, also tucked into a corner in the front.

At this point, we still didn't know exactly what was going on, but at least we knew who the players were. Elaina wanted to get close enough to overhear their conversation, but I didn't think it was a good idea. I thought she might be spotted, and I felt like Lurch, and even Herbert Long, were unpredictable and possibly dangerous.

Agent Marek had what I thought was still a dangerous but better idea. She took a mask out of her coat pocket and said she would put it on and go over near their table after their dinner had been served. Teresa felt that they would be somewhat preoccupied with the food and her mask made it less likely that Herbert Long or Yi Peng would recognize her. Besides, she reminded us that three of the people at the table were Chinese speakers, and only one of us was.

We agreed to give agent Marek's plan a try and proceeded to enjoy our entrées. The short ribs were excellent, and Henry and Teresa were happy with their salmon. During dinner, Elaina revealed that the phone call she had received earlier was from the Gang Task Force Detective José Santos. He wants to see us at the 12th District Station on South Blue Island Avenue tomorrow morning. He added that he only wanted to see me and my partner. I felt a little uneasy about that part, but she figured it was better just to let everyone know.

Agent Chan said that was not a problem. He understood about territorial issues. He and Agent Marek planned on spending the morning at their office. Apparently, they had plenty of other work to keep them busy. Elaina thanked him for being so understanding. Without looking their way, Henry Chan lowered his voice and stated that Herbert Long's party had just been served their entrées. Agent Marek nodded, slipped on her mask, and quietly got up from the table. She blended right in with a stream of people walking around the dining room going to and from the bar, the bathrooms and the outer decks. She wasn't the only one wearing a mask either. Many people continued wearing them as a precaution against COVID and other types of infection.

While Teresa was gone, Agent Chan told us about some of the background information that he and Agent Marek had gleaned from FBI databases and intelligence reports concerning all of the dinner guests at the N. Astor Street. party and, more specifically, the guests on the Odyssey that night.

It seems that none of them had any significant criminal records. He reported that Li Zen from Shanghai Power was a bit of a scofflaw, often ringing up large numbers of parking tickets before having one of his lawyers negotiate a settlement and then beginning the process over again. Also, Dominic Blasi had a couple of minor problems as a juvenile that did not result in any record. Otherwise, there were no legal problems or obvious financial difficulties among them.

A few minutes later, Teresa Marek came back to our table, removed her mask, and excitedly but quietly told us what she had learned. She began by saying that she was able to stand near the door to the lower outside deck, which was only a few feet from their table. She had needed to keep her back to the table so she couldn't hear every word clearly but had heard a lot.

She said that the conversation was animated, almost heated. In English, she heard Francine Vito, Harriet Bingham and Li Zen

108

encouraging Dominic Blasi to join them in some kind of important venture. They all were confident that the opportunity was too good to pass up. But Blasi was clearly balking. When he told the group that he couldn't go along with it, Herbert Long entered the conversation and said that he thought it was unfortunate but that Mr. Blasi had the right to make that decision. He then said nevertheless he wished him well.

Herbert Long then turned his head to Security Director Yi Peng and Li Zen and spoke in Chinese with a very different tone. He said that the disagreeable one, as he called him, was a big problem that now must be dealt with. Long asked Yi Peng to notify the boss that action was needed right away. He wanted him to tell the boss to set the plan in motion. Yi Peng took out his phone and began texting, and Herbert Long started talking about how good the food was and asking the guests if they wanted refills on their drinks.

I began to feel that I had stayed there a little too long, and when a group of people walked in from the lower deck, I joined them and came back to our table.

An announcement that the dessert bar was now open interrupted our conversation and prompted dinner guests to begin lining up for a selection of melons, strawberries, and sweet baked goods. Having quite a sweet tooth myself, I had to resist the urge to go up there and get a couple of brownies. So, we all kept our seats and watched as our people of interest and everyone else visited the dessert bar.

After what Teresa Marek reported about what she overheard at their table, we became hyper-vigilant. We didn't know if there were other accomplices among the dinner crowd. We had to wonder whether there were assassins placed at tables inside the dining room. No one wanted to be paranoid, but with the way things had been going, we knew that we needed to be ready for anything.

While most of the guests took turns at the dessert bar, including Dominic Blasi, Francine Vito, Harriet Bingham, and even Herbert

Long, we evaluated everybody, including the few who stayed at their table. The families with school-age children were quickly dismissed, but that still left dozens of adults in groups of two, four, and six.

We didn't notice anything that raised a red flag. We also knew that was no reason to relax, but it didn't give us any direction or focus either. Another announcement informed us that the Navy Pier fireworks would be starting soon and invited people to watch from their seats or enjoy it from the upper or lower decks and recommended the upper deck for the best view.

Soon after that, many in the crowd began moving toward the back for the bathrooms and the upper deck. A few headed out the front to the lower deck, and some, including Herbert Long and his party, remained seated.

We now had a mostly unobstructed view of their table, which was good, but that meant they had the same view of us. Fortunately, no one at their table appeared to notice us or anyone else. They seemed engaged in conversation among themselves. Nevertheless, Elaina and I kept our backs to them and relied on Chan and Marek to keep an eye on them. After a few minutes, just as we could hear that the fireworks had begun, Agent Marek reported that Yi Peng took a phone call that seemed to cause some movement by the group. They all stood up except the shadowy Head of Consulate Security and Dominic Blasi.

Herbert Long proceeded to lead the rest of the group through the dining room on the pathway opposite from our side of the room toward the back and presumably to the upper deck. Considering that most of the group were headed up and that there would be a much larger group of people up there, Elaina, Henry and Teresa would follow them, and I would stay with Lurch and Dominic Blasi.

After waiting about a minute, Elaina led the agents toward the upper deck, and I kept my eyes trained on Yi Peng and Blasi. A couple more drinks were delivered to their table, and they clinked glasses and seemed to be having a grand old time. By the sound of it, the fireworks show was in full swing. Yi Peng suddenly stood up, grabbed his drink, and motioned for Blasi to follow him. They walked out the nearby front entrance and onto the lower deck.

As my partners nonchalantly rose from the table to discreetly follow Herbert Long and several of his guests up to the main outer deck, I strode slowly through the dining room and straight outside to the lower deck. There I joined a group of about a dozen people enjoying a drink and watching the fireworks coming out from Navy Pier to our left.

Yi Peng and Dominic Blasi stood gazing up at the explosions in the night sky at the railing to my left. Nothing seemed out of place for the moment. I noticed boats cruising past us after coming out of marinas on the Chicago River, mostly on their way to the playpen outside of Ohio Street Beach north of the Pier. It was a popular spot where boats lashed up together to party and on this night to watch the fireworks which rose over Olive Park from Navy Pier.

I watched some of the pleasure boats pass by, looking for a familiar face but didn't see one. My attention had only been diverted for a few seconds, but when I turned my attention back to Yi Peng and Dominic Blasi, I was surprised to see that Blasi was alone by the outer rail. The mysterious Lurch was nowhere in sight. For some reason, this struck me as being alarming.

I turned my head back to my right to survey the group of partiers that were all preoccupied with each other or watching the booming fireworks display, which was picking up in frequency and firepower. I usually enjoy fireworks as much as the next guy, but in this case, they were just a pain in the ass distraction. Maybe even a diversion.

Peering through the small crowd on the deck, I spotted something that made the hair on my neck stand at attention. There were two grappling hooks attached to the rail that had not been there a minute before.

In an instant, my alarm became a frightening reality. Two diminutive nimble figures covered in black began swinging themselves over the rail and onto the deck. I instinctively felt my right hip expecting to reach my Beretta, which unfortunately was in a shoulder holster shit! I had lost a precious second, and anyway, it occurred to me that I couldn't fire into that crowd, and there was no time. They were already on deck, and they had pistols fitted with silencers in their hands.

I bolted the 10 feet between myself and Blasi, inadvertently knocking a young couple out of the way spilling their drinks on them and me. Blasi saw me coming at the last second but didn't have time to react. I was on him in a flash and picked him up from his groin and, in one move, tossed him over the side. I bolted up and over the wall and could hear screams and gasps from the passengers amid the symphony of exploding fireworks overhead.

Hitting the water awkwardly, I was submerged for a few seconds before emerging, hoping to see Blasi nearby. He was a little ways behind me and struggling a little bit to stay above the water. I yelled to him to take off his coat as I wiggled out of mine. At the same time, I heard the pfft pfft of bullets fired from pistols with silencers splashing into the water around us. The ship was moving slowly past us and might have caused the shooters to miss. But they weren't missing by much.

Suddenly the shooting stopped. That was good. But then I saw the two ninja-like figures gliding down the grappling ladders like spider monkeys. And, I noticed that there was a sleek twin-engine powerboat pulling up to collect them. That was bad. Just then, another speedboat appeared out of nowhere from the other side of the Odyssey, passing the ninjas who were just getting on board. It was Morgan Latner and Henrique Sanchez. This was beyond good.

112

They swiftly pulled us up on board, and without saying anything, Latner took the wheel and gunned the engines. The fireworks show was exploding into the grand finale, but I could still hear the faint sounds of more gunshots whizzing by us. I reached for my doused Beretta, hoping it would fire. I got off several shots, and Detective Sanchez joined in firing at the ninjas in the pursuing boat.

Then my gun jammed, and I yelled to Latner to give me his Glock. As I took it from him, I pushed Dominic Blasi to the bottom of the boat, rather forcefully ordering him to stay down. I resumed firing, but it was nearly impossible to hit anything while being bounced up and down in the choppy water at a very high rate of speed. Luckily our pursuers had the same problem.

We took a course out into the Lake, going around the Jardine Waterworks and past Ohio Street Beach. There were often Chicago Police Department boats out in that area, but we didn't see one. Morgan had gotten on the radio right away and was talking or yelling through all the noise to a police dispatcher. We had to steer clear of the playpen for fear of putting any innocent boaters in harm's way.

Latner was an experienced and adept pilot, and his maneuverings kept the pursuers lagging a little behind us, but their boat was as powerful as ours, and we couldn't shake them. So, we kept shooting at them, and they kept shooting at us with the same lousy accuracy on both sides.

The cat and mouse shooting exercise continued for a while until, abruptly, our boat began to slow and then stopped altogether. Morgan yelled that something in the electrical system shorted out, and we weren't going anywhere for a while. This was very, very bad. I didn't know what kind of firepower the ninjas might have on board, but we were now sitting ducks.

The fireworks show now in the distance had ended with a flourish, and it was eerily quiet all of a sudden. We hunkered down into our boat, and both sides kept firing. Now the shots were hitting their mark much better. Bullets pinged into the side of our vessel as ours slammed into theirs. Then I saw the thing I was afraid of most. The ninjas were now holding automatic rifles. They each got off a burst as we huddled on the floor.

Then we heard a booming sound of a different kind off in the distance. It was the booming foghorn of an emergency Chicago Police Department boat, coming toward us from the north. It had probably been patrolling near Oak Street Beach when it heard Latner's call. The shooting stopped. We listened to the attacking boat start its engines and speed away out into the darkness of the Lake.

Slowly everyone picked themselves up off the floor in time to catch a glimpse of the pursuers race off farther out and disappear into the night. The Chicago PD boat pulled alongside, and I couldn't help myself from letting out a joyous yeeeee haaaaa! Latner, Sanchez and I exchanged some high-fives, and I exclaimed, "I think they were the same little jagoffs that I ran into at N. Astor Street in the alley."

Our elation was a little short-lived after we noticed how much water Morgan's boat was taking on. The officers waved for us to get into their boat and quickly hooked up a towline as Capt. Latner reluctantly disembarked. Officer Ron Stanton got us some towels and asked, "What the hell was that all about?"

I responded, "Have you ever tried the dinner cruise from Navy Pier? You really should. It's a hell of a rush!"

Then I turned to Dominic Blasi and said, "Sorry, Blasi. Sit down and enjoy the ride back. We need to talk."

Chapter 12

On the way back to the Marine Safety Station at Navy Pier, where the 45-foot patrol boat that picked us up is kept, I had a chance to interview Dominic Blasi about precisely what preceded the attack on the Odyssey. After changing into a dry pair of shorts and a T-shirt provided by the officers on board, the conversation got serious.

Blasi declined a change of clothes, and Latner and Sanchez were damp but not soaked, so they passed on dry clothes as well. We sat down in the back of the boat, and I started by asking Blasi to tell me how the dinner party came about. He said that he got a call from investment banker, Bingham, inviting him to the dinner cruise to hear about an incredible business opportunity. It was all a little vague, but he knew Harriet Bingham to be a serious player in large projects, so he decided to attend.

Blasi said that at first, the dinner seemed pleasant and just a typical meeting among successful business people. He had met all of the other guests except the big scary guy, Yi Peng, recently at the N. Astor Street dinner, so everything was fine until the guy from Argyle Street, Herbert Long, who seemed to be in charge, began explaining the purpose of the dinner.

Dominic started laughing and shook his head a little, and said, "Somehow, they were under the impression that I was a little shady and open to a proposition that was illegal if the payoff was big enough. Long was unclear about what it was, so I just kept listening."

"Everyone there seemed to be on the inside of what was going on except me. Whatever they had planned would involve large-scale shipping from Shanghai to ports in the US, particularly New Orleans. This was going to be facilitated by Li Zen from Shanghai Power and Technologies. Products would be brought in by Francine

Vito at North American Importers and distributed all over the US. Harriet Bingham was to arrange for large-scale funding, and they were counting on me to launder the profits from this venture."

I asked Blasi if he knew what Yi Peng's part was in the whole thing. Dominic wasn't sure, but he thought it was implied that the Chinese Consulate in Chicago was entirely behind the venture. He said that the whole thing was starting to make him nervous. He went on to say, "It seemed like a big drug deal to me. Definitely not something that I would be interested in, but I tried to tap dance around, making a commitment without actually saying no. The whole thing made me uneasy, and that Yi Peng guy was downright scary."

"At some point, Herbert Long abruptly changed the subject, and we finished our dinners and ordered another round of drinks before going out to watch the fireworks. The consulate guy, Peng, pulled me aside, and we went out to the front while the others followed Herbert Long to the back."

"When we got to the lower deck, he tried his best to make me feel at ease by saying that he understood my hesitation to join the project and that it was no problem. There were no hard feelings. Somehow, it didn't make me feel more at ease. He excused himself to go to the bathroom just as the fireworks really got underway. I felt safer after he left, but that didn't last long. Before I knew it, you were throwing me overboard, and we were being shot at and chased by some crazy ninja hitmen. And now here we are."

It wasn't long before we were pulling into the side of Navy Pier. We all sincerely thanked the officers who saved our asses and got off the boat and onto the Pier. I grabbed my still wet clothes, holster and gun, and cell phone. Blasi and I had parked at the lot right there at the Pier, and as we all walked to our cars, I asked Blasi if he had a safe place to go for a few days. He responded that he could go to his uncle's home in River Forest. He smiled and said that his uncle was the kind of guy that would know how to handle something like this. He laughed again and said, "You don't want to know."

I had a pretty good idea of what he meant, but he was right. I didn't want to know. I did, however, want to know where Elaina and the FBI agents were, and I knew that I needed a beer.

My phone was a lost cause for the time being, so I turned it off and asked Morgan Latner to give Elaina a call. It turns out they were still waiting for us at the Pier near where the Odyssey unloaded. I asked Morgan to tell them to meet us at Timothy O'Toole's in 15 minutes.

We walked Dominic Blasi to his black Mercedes convertible with tan interior. I asked him to stay in touch, and Morgan Latner gave him a card. He got in and said, "Thanks, Detective Fallon. But you still owe me a sport coat," and laughed as he drove out of the lot with a wave. I wasn't sure about anything in this case, but my instincts told me he was okay.

Fortunately, my key fob was still working, so we climbed into my black-on-black Chevy Camaro. Okay, it wasn't a Mercedes, I thought to myself, but it was mine, and I love it.

I found a halfway legal spot, on N. Fairbanks Street, and we walked down the stairs into the bar at Timothy O'Toole's. The others were already settled in at a table for six, and we happily joined them. It was nice to take a break and enjoy the fact that we were all alive and well, except for Koz, of course.

I called Zilene Baker for an update at the hospital. She was still there but was getting ready to leave for the night. She and Koz's wife had just been given a briefing by the chief surgeon, who was pleased to report that the surgeries were successful. The prognosis was good for a complete recovery, but it would be a long process, and he would remain in intensive care for a while.

Our server Tracy delivered a couple of pitchers of Miller, and we filled our glasses and clinked them together in a toast to our partner, Frank Kozlowski. Yeah, he could be a real jerk, but he was our jerk, and we all cared about him and were greatly relieved to hear the good news.

Tracy kept the pictures coming, and after a couple of hours of recapping the events of the evening and the last couple of days, we called it a night and agreed to meet up in the morning at the station.

Outside, the warm summer evening was refreshing. The air was dry, and the gentle breeze was soothing. It was enough to almost sweep away the harrowing experience out on Lake Michigan that night and everything else that was happening in this crazy case. Almost. Morgan and Henrique needed to come with me, so we said goodbye to the others and climbed back into my Camaro.

Henrique wanted to go to the station to get his car, and Morgan had left his at Montrose Harbor. We enjoyed the ride up Lakeshore Drive and soon were pulling into the parking lot at the harbor.

"Thanks for coming to the rescue tonight, buddy." I said sincerely as he pulled his lanky body out of the car.

"No problem, Jack," he replied, "except I'm not exactly sure how to explain all of this to my dad and brother. Looks like our boating season was even shorter than usual this summer." He said with a laugh.

"I am really sorry about that, man. If you have any repairs that aren't covered, count me in for my share."

"I'll keep that in mind, Jack," he chuckled. "We have great insurance, and I'll put a claim in with the Department for the deductible. My dad will be too happy that I didn't get shot, and my brother will give me crap for a while. He will enjoy that almost as much as he enjoys boating anyway."

When I got home, my apartment never looked better to me. I experienced an almost overwhelming feeling of appreciation just to be there alive and well. I put on some Nora Jones music and laid down on my couch to just close my eyes and wander away amid mindless thoughts. I woke up after a deep but restless sleep. The sounds of whizzing bullets and the foghorn blast from the police boat kept coming back. The pounding bouncing feeling of Morgan's powerboat felt so real; it eventually woke me up at around 5:00 AM.

From the windows in my living room, the sky was lit up with bands of pink streaming across the horizon. I recalled the words of the poet, Homer, who called it *the rosy-fingered dawn.* I thought that guy really nailed it.

Soon I was wide awake. After a shave and a shower, it was time for a quick breakfast of soft-boiled eggs toasted Catherine Clark bread and orange juice. I watched the morning news while I ate and was happy to learn that there was little mention about what had happened on the dinner cruise. They simply said there had been a report of a disturbance on one of Navy Pier's cruise ships, and more details would be reported when they got them. I hoped they never would.

When I finished the quick breakfast, I turned my attention to the day ahead. The weather forecast was terrific, but I knew that the forecast for our case was cloudy at best. A storm seemed to be looming, and I needed to be ready for it.

My thoughts turned to my service weapon—the trusty 9 mm Beretta. After the soaking last night, it had jammed on me. I couldn't have that. So, I decided to break it down and give it a thorough cleaning and make sure it was totally dry before putting it back together with a brand-new clip. I put a couple of extra clips in my tan cotton sport coat that I had picked out for this bright summer day, along with khaki slacks and a light blue short-sleeved Oxford shirt with a Navy-blue tie with gold stripes.

I gave Zilene Baker a call and learned that she was already at the hospital with her partner. He was sleeping, and she said that she had managed to talk his wife into going home to get some sleep.

She was going to stay with Koz until Anna came back. "No problem," I said, "take all the time you need. We've got this."

Actually, I wasn't so sure that we had it, but what the hell. Zilene didn't need to hear that. I checked in with my partner, and Elaina said she was already on the way to the station. I hung up with her and soon was on my way to work with my gun and badge on my belt where they belonged.

At the station, I was relieved not to see any media trucks or reporters. There always seemed to be sensational stories in Chicago, and I guessed that our case wasn't sexy enough that day. For whatever the reason, I was grateful. It was one less thing to deal with.

Once inside, I was impressed to see Elaina, Morgan Henrique and our FBI partners already at work. I laid out the plan for the day, which was that Agents Chan and Marek would go with Latner and Sanchez to follow up on interviews with the guests from the dinner cruise other than Dominic Blasi. I realized that Yi Peng would probably be unwilling to cooperate. There was nothing we could do about that. He had diplomatic immunity, and he knew it.

Elaina and I headed down to Pilsen to meet with Gang Detectives José Santos and Devin Bulger. But first, we would report to Lieut. Whitehead about the events of the previous evening and our plans for the day.

So, after checking messages and returning a few phone calls for about 1/2 an hour, we were informed that the Lieutenant was in his office and ready to see us. We spent about 10 minutes catching Whitehead up to speed, and then we signed out our Chevy Impala and were on our way to Pilsen.

This time the ride to Elaina's home neighborhood was quieter and more serious. I was still pretty amazed at the colorful visuals that pervade Pilsen, along with the smells and sounds of Mexico. This case weighed heavily on the whole team. Every member had been in the line of fire at least once. Koz had been shot twice and was still in intensive care after surgery, and Elaina was basically in mourning. She is a real professional, but I could tell it had taken its toll on her.

Our meeting place, the District 12 Station, was a more modern structure of steel and glass which stood out in contrast to the Czechoslovakian and German architecture, that predominates in the neighborhood.

We reported to the desk Sargent, a middle-aged woman named Officer Gutierrez. Elaina introduced her to me as Millie. She was very pleasant and seemed to be well-known to my partner. She called the detectives then directed us up the stairs to room 207.

The station was a typically bustling place full of citizens, officers, and detectives, coming and going and creating a cacophony of voices and ringing phones. Room 207 was the home of the Gang Unit and was comprised of six desks with computers and phones. Santos and Bulger were sitting in adjacent desks and were the only ones present at the time.

Santos waved us in and pointed to chairs set up for us in front of them. He said hello in a low but somehow menacing voice. I had to admit to myself that these guys were unnerving. He smiled at Elaina and asked her if she was okay and if she needed anything. She thanked him and said that she was good and would see them tomorrow at Chico's funeral.

With that out of the way, we turned our attention to the matters at hand. Detective Bulger started the conversation by telling us that they had been receiving reports from several sources that there have been ongoing talks between high-level players in several Latino and Chinese heavyweight gangs, and people from the Chinese Consulate. It wasn't clear to their sources exactly who the Chinese players were, but they were sure that the Latinos involved were serious guys.

The subject of the talks was heroin distribution. The Chinese were offering a new heavy volume supply of cheap heroin brought in directly from China to the US in shipping containers, and promising that their price would beat the Mexican cartels since they didn't have to get the product across the US Mexican border. It basically would cut the cartels out as middlemen. The savings would be significant, but so would the risk of going up against the Mexican drug lords.

Detective Santos took over seamlessly and noted that a couple of their informants were convinced that the Latino gangs were just stringing the Chinese along and had no intention of actually doing business with them. The thought was that they were hoping to get some upfront money or heroin from the Chinese and then just blow them off. They weren't afraid of them, but they were afraid of the Mexican cartels. They were well aware of what they were capable of.

"So, at some point, the shit could really hit the fan on this one if the Chinese retaliate." Santos continued. "Pilsen is right fucking next to Chinatown. They usually stay away from each other, but this could change that. We need to put a stop to the whole damn deal if we can."

I decided to interrupt briefly to ask a question that had been on my mind since Elaina mentioned this meeting at the dinner cruise. "Do you mind letting us know why you didn't want the FBI agents to attend our meeting?"

The way Santos looked at me made me start to regret the interruption. "I was getting to that detective." He explained that their informants also had heard that the Chinese were bragging that they had some high-level FBI protection. They didn't think that it involved Chan or Marek, but it was someone that they reported to.

Apparently, they had been tipped off about the agent that was planted in one of Herbert Long's restaurants. She had witnessed some of the meetings with Latino gang leaders and Chinese and

Vietnamese players from Argyle Street. Since she spoke both Chinese and Vietnamese, she had overheard enough to pass on her suspicions that some kind of significant drug deal was being discussed. She was right, and that cost her —her life."

Santos wrapped it up by saying he hoped the information had been useful and offered to help in any way they could.

We all stood up, and I shook hands with each of them. I am a pretty good size guy with a nice firm grip on a handshake, but these guys had a way of shaking hands and looking you in the eye that just screamed out, *don't fuck with me.*

On the way out the door, Santos told Elaina that he would see her in the morning. Elaina stopped and looked back at them. "Any leads on finding that little shit on the red bike?" She wanted to know.

Santo's eyes flashed, and Bulger smiled and added, "We are working on it." in such a way that it seemed like a foregone conclusion

Chapter 13

On the way out of Pilsen, we decided to swing by the hospital to check on Koz. It also gave us a little time to discuss what we knew and didn't know about the case.

First, we knew that we had a group of 14 people that seemed to be part of whatever was going on here. Four Chinese Consulate officials, eight high-powered business people, and two art experts. One of the consulate officials had been murdered, and one narrowly escaped a murder attempt. Among the eight business people, two have also been killed, and two have been the subject of assassination attempts.

It was uncertain where the two art experts and the theft of the Egg of Chaos fit into the picture. It was also unclear whether the remaining consulate and business people were targets or suspects. We also didn't know whether the murders and the planning for a mega heroin deal were even connected to the art heist. Was someone going to try to sell the artifact to help fund the heroin plan, or was it completely unrelated? We just didn't know.

Elaina was listening intently and then responded. "Jack, we need to find a way to flush these people out. The consulate officials are a real problem. They can hide behind diplomatic immunity, and the others are savvy hard-nosed business types, who won't put up with an intense interrogation. The artsy guys probably would come in for an interrogation, but at this point, I'm not sure it would be worth it."

"I totally agree." I said. "I think I may have an idea that might do it. I will call the Lieutenant and see if he will meet us at Stroger Hospital. This is going to require his go-ahead and a little subterfuge." I laughed and asked her if she was down with that.

Elaina seemed to brighten up a little for the first time in a couple of days. "You bet!" She answered with a smile. "Whatever it takes, partner."

With that, I began to put my plan into action. A couple of calls were made. One was to Lieutenant Whitehead, who agreed to meet us at the hospital. He said that he was planning to see Detective Kozlowski anyway, and he was open to suggestions on how to solve this mess. Even though the media had not focused on our case as much as some other things going on in the city, Whitehead was under heavy pressure from CPD Command, who were feeling the heat from the Mayor.

My next call went to Morgan Latner. I told him an old school Catholic white lie that there was nothing new from the gang unit detectives. They had just wanted to see how Elaina was holding up after the shooting of her CI and friend Chico at the park in Pilsen. We also made plans to meet later that night, where everything would be explained. Keeping him in the dark was necessary for now.

Once we got to the hospital, and were able to park about 1/2 a block from the front entrance, we found Zilene and Anna sitting outside the intensive care unit. I asked how Koz was doing and was informed that he was under heavy sedation and painkillers as well as being on a ventilator and getting intravenous feeding.

I told Detective Baker that the Lieutenant was on his way and that we would like her to join our meeting with him.

First, though, I wanted to go in to at least be with Koz for a while, the lady directing traffic from her desk in the lobby said only two of us could go in at a time. So, Elaina and I were shown into the unit and led to our partner's room.

He was totally hooked up. We each took a different side of his bed and just stood silently for a minute. Then I decided to talk to him just in case he could hear us, even subconsciously. I began telling him about our meeting with Santos and Bulger, as well as about what we knew concerning the case. To our surprise, his eyes opened up, and he looked right at me. His blue eyes were clear, and there was some of the old Kozlowski fire in them. That look had often been accompanied by a caustic remark, and the thought of it made me smile.

"You old dog," I said with a broad grin on my face. "Here we all thought you were seriously injured, and you were just sandbagging us." I could tell that he had started to laugh a little, but then he grimaced in pain. I said, "sorry, buddy. I'm just glad to see you are hanging in there. Keep up the good work."

Elaina placed her hand on his arm and asked him if there was anything we could do for him. He shook his head ever so slightly, indicating no. I then asked him if we could borrow Zilene for a while. We needed her to help catch the bastards that did this to him. This time he nodded a little more demonstrably. It was definitely a yes.

I put my hand on his shoulder and told him, "Thanks, big guy. You are still a part of this case. When I see Whitehead in a few minutes, I will tell him that you can still work effectively even without being able to speak. And I'm going to ask him if we can keep you muzzled even after you fully recover and get back to work."

This time he couldn't help himself from laughing, and I could only imagine what those bright blue eyes were saying to me. His nurse, a short slender young woman named Briony, who had been observing us and his vital signs, intervened and said, "Okay, that's enough of that. You've got him a little overstimulated. He needs to be resting."

We saw Lieutenant Whitehead sitting and talking quietly with Anna in the waiting area. We sat nearby but didn't interject ourselves into their conversation. The quiet time was welcome, and it continued even after Whitehead and Anna went into intensive care to see Koz. It seems that Elaina and Zilene were just as happy to have a quiet moment as I was.

Twenty minutes later, Anna and the Lieutenant emerged from intensive care, and after sharing a few last words, Anna went back in, and Whitehead turned his attention to us. He sat down among us, and since there was no one else around, I decided it was as good a place and time as any; to lay out my plan.

First, I relayed the information provided by the gang detectives in Pilsen. Then I got to our idea that Elaina and I thought, could draw out the people responsible for the murders and possibly the theft of the ancient artifact.

Lieutenant Whitehead was very concerned about the heroin element and the possible flare-up of significant violence between Asian and Latin gangs. It was something that had never really happened in Chicago and definitely something no one wanted to see. But he was especially troubled by the idea that there was a rogue special agent within the FBI, that was a player in this murderous scheme to flood Chicago with inexpensive heroin from China.

I could see that he was uncomfortable and a little overwhelmed by what he had just learned. He said he was tempted to blow the lid off the whole thing by going up the chain of command at CPD or even going public. Neither of which I thought was a good idea. I had to calm him down and convince him that there was another way. That we could handle this.

"Lieutenant, hear me out," I began. "There's no doubt this case is complicated because we have Chinese diplomats who can shield themselves with diplomatic immunity. And we have a fairly high-ranking FBI special agent playing ball with some corrupt Chinese officials. We need to find out who the bad guys at the consulate and FBI headquarters are, before this goes any further. And I think I know how to do that."

Whitehead groaned and leaned back, saying, "Okay, detective, this better be good."

"I think I have an idea that can work and work right away. We will need to keep this plan completely under our hats. Only our team can be in on the whole thing. Lieutenant, I need you to find us an officer to come to the station tomorrow to pretend to be a neighbor of the townhouse owners on N. Astor Street. Detectives Latner and Sanchez will interview him along with Agents Chan and Marek. He will reveal that the townhouse owners will be coming back from Europe on Sunday. And oh, this may not be important, but they told me a while ago that they had installed hidden cameras inside the townhouse that were nearly impossible to detect. Just thought you might want to know."

"Agents Chan and Marek need to be instructed to keep this information top-secret and tell only their immediate supervisor, Special Agent Manion. They will also be informed that the CSI team expects to be finished with the townhouse by no later than Saturday late afternoon, and that the security patrol will be taken off by us at that time."

"Zilene, I need you to reinterview Li Zen from Shanghai Power and Technology. You need to focus on what he knows about the trafficking of ancient artworks, specifically the Egg of Chaos. Convince him that we think finding the artifact is the key to solving the case. Ask him what he knows about our two art experts and whether he thinks they did anything suspicious at the dinner party on Saturday night. Make him feel comfortable and that we appreciate his help."

"Elaina will contact Detectives Santos and Bulger and ask them to contact their confidential informants and pump them for information regarding stolen artwork. Really put some pressure on them. Make it seem like that was our major focus. Who knows, maybe that will get back to the right Chinese players at the consulate."

"I intend to focus on the Southside Chinatown connection tomorrow, and Elaina has some personal business in Pilsen in the morning. She will then join up with me after that."

"If this goes the way I see it, we will be ready for them on Saturday night. Lieutenant, we will need you to coordinate with CSI and the patrol units, and I will keep our teammates positioned where I need them."

Lieutenant Whitehead sighed and gave me a look that knocked me back. "There are a lot of ways that this could go sideways, detective. If I go along with this, my ass will be on the line, and yours is right there with me." What followed was a long, painful pause, during which his penetrating brown eyes never left me. I felt the heat, but I didn't look away.

Finally, he broke the silence. "Okay, Fallon. I am going to give you your head on this one. I'm putting my faith in you. And for God's sake, don't fuck this up."

I felt like jumping up and giving him a high five, but I didn't even smile. I simply said seriously, "I will not let you down."

Whitehead stood up, and his massive 6'6" frame loomed over us. "We all have our work to do," he said sternly. "Let's get going. Take care of yourselves out there and keep me in the loop." And in a few long strides, he was gone.

Zilene Baker decided to stay for a while but said she would try to schedule an interview with Li Zen asap.

Elaina and I headed back to the station to put in some work on other cases. We all have extensive caseloads, but this one had taken priority for the past six days. On the way, Elaina contacted Detective Santos, who promised to take care of their end. I had no doubt that he would.

We spent a couple of hours trying unsuccessfully to catch up on our cases. We barely had time to make a dent on a couple of files. It was business as usual.

The time flew by, and soon Elaina needed to go home to her family and then help with final arrangements for Chico's funeral. And I needed to get going to meet Morgan Latner at Harry Caray's on W. Kinzie Street.

Soon I was walking through the double doors under the green canopied entranceway to another one of my favorite restaurants, Harry Caray's Italian Steakhouse and Sports Bar. Latner wasn't there yet, so I walked into the long rectangular barroom with tables placed to the right side along the windows, facing North to Dearborn Street and took a seat at the classic saloon-like bar on the left.

Two familiar faces were behind the bar handling the moderately busy action with ease. Frank and Lee had been there for years and were real pros. I sat in Lee's section, and he greeted me with a bowl of their signature homemade chips and a bottle of Heineken. For some reason, that was always what I drank at Harry Caray's. It was partially because they didn't offer Miller High Life, only Miller Lite. I enjoyed a lot of different beers, just not light beers.

My colleague and good friend Morgan Latner arrived shortly thereafter and took the seat to my right. I put the chips between us and tried hard to stop eating them. They are very addicting. He ordered a Goose Island 312.

We caught up on the most recent developments in the case, and I explained what I needed him to do. He understood immediately and liked the plan except for the part he had in playing a role that he saw as more acting than detecting. He also wasn't happy about not being in, on the intended action on N. Astor Street., but I made sure that he knew he and Henrique would play a critical role in the deception.

Our beers went down quickly, and Lee brought two more before checking whether we were ready to order some food. We were more than ready. I ordered one of their specialties, Chicken Vesuvio, and Morgan went with the Lasagna.

While we enjoyed the beers and waited for our food, we covered some of our usual subjects, those being Chicago's sports teams, our families, and love interests. Morgan had been with the same girlfriend, Tina, for the last two years and seemed happy. She had an apartment in Evanston, which wasn't too far from his place in Edgewater. They had known each other since their days at Evanston High School but didn't start dating until much later.

He knew about my infatuation with Emma Merlin. He had been there the night I met her at The Green Mill in April, and had witnessed my trancelike reaction. I told him about our abbreviated date at her art exhibit and how this fucking case had messed up my chance to meet up with her at the after-party.

Morgan laughed as guys do at news like that. "That's life in the big city, huh, Jack," he said, enjoying it a little too much for my liking. I playfully pushed him and said, "Thanks for your support, pal, and I thought you had my back." He laughed again and answered. "I'm sure you'll get another shot at it. Just let me know if you need any help with that." I responded with a mocked serious "*Fuck you,*" and then our banter was interrupted by the sight of one of Harry Caray's white-coated waiters delivering our food to Lee for service at the bar. Everything was laid out before us, including copious amounts of their fresh-baked bread, cups of soft butter, and cloth table linens accompanied by two more beers.

While we ate, Morgan inquired about how my dad and siblings were doing. We had gotten to know each other's immediate families at parties, BBQs, and outings on Lake Michigan. I mentioned that my dad was still going strong as the First Assistant in the Cook County Public Defender's Office. He was still conducting trials and taking on some of the most challenging cases. Older brother Barry was doing well, still working as one of the managers at Timothy

O'Toole's, and sister Molly was happy in academia being a Professor of History at Northwestern University in Evanston.

When I asked him about his family, he answered that all was well. His dad was still running Evanston's Park District and had no intention of retiring. His mom was an account manager at a thriving software company located in downtown Evanston, and his older brother Marcus was still working as an accountant with the firm downtown on LaSalle Street and living with his wife and two kids in Lincoln Park.

I couldn't help myself from asking him how they all reacted to the fact that their prized speedboat was now full of bullet holes and being held as evidence. He laughed even harder this time and said that their response was about what he had expected. His parents were so happy that he was unharmed that they hardly inquired about the boat. His brother, on the other hand, feigned outrage at the damage and said something like, "Aren't you guys supposed to step in front of things like that to protect private property?"

This time I laughed, knowing his brother's dry sense of humor. We finished our delicious meals and were ready for one of their excellent desserts. As usual, I ordered the tiramisu, the best in the city, and Morgan decided on some Eli's cheesecake. We both added coffee, and together they topped off another satisfying visit to Harry's. We settled up and said our farewells to Lee and Frank. "See you guys next time."

We left and entered into the warm breezy air of a glorious Chicago summer night. On my ride home along Lakeshore Drive, the clear night sky revealed a mesmerizing nearly full moon hanging out over Belmont Harbor.

Just as I was beginning to enjoy the moment a little too much, the buzz of my phone snapped me out of it. I tapped answer on my screen and was surprised to hear the sultry tones of Lily Mai Tong's voice. Hearing her say, "Hello, Detective Fallon" reminded me of how sensual her handshake at the nightclub had been, and I started getting excited. *Wow,* I thought. *This could be dangerous.*

She went on to say that she needed to see me and hoped I would come to Chinatown in the morning. Since I had already planned on going down there, I immediately agreed. The truth is, I would've found a way to get there regardless. We agreed on a plan, and I proceeded home.

My sleep that night wasn't as restful as I had anticipated, but my dreams were much sweeter.

Chapter 14

Friday morning, I awoke after a deep refreshing sleep. The sun was shining at 6 AM, and it was going to be another spectacular summer day in my city. Whatever else awaited me, I was going to savor a peaceful start.

I lingered in a hot shower for as long as I could justify, and after I decided it was time to get to work, I blasted myself with a cold soak that helped snap me back to reality.

The plan for the morning was to meet Lily Mai Tong at Chinatown Square, where she would be participating in a Tai Chi class between eight and nine. So, I decided on a light breakfast of frosted flakes and hazelnut vanilla coffee from my Keurig.

It was another day for a light-colored suit with a white short-sleeved Oxford shirt and maroon tie with gold stripes and comfortable brown Rockport walking shoes.

The trip down Lakeshore Drive presented pleasant views of the parks and beaches already beginning to fill up with swimmers, walkers, runners and bikers. It was great to be young and so alive in this incredible social experiment called Chicago.

It wasn't far to Chinatown, and soon after I got on S. Archer Avenue, the Chinatown Square appeared on my right. I drove past the central plaza, where I noticed a group of about 20 people moving in a graceful slow-motion dancelike rhythm. I recognized it as being Tai Chi, but that was about as far as my knowledge of it went. I continued past them and pulled into a strip mall-type parking area with plenty of open spaces.

Walking over to the square's open plaza, I again realized just how little I knew about this historic and vibrant part of the city. I had always been of a curious mind, and I was determined to continue to learn more about what this magnificent melting pot had to offer.

When I came across the Tai Chi group, I stood a little ways away and just watched the fluid, effortless movements and became mesmerized by the gentle motions and soothing sounds of silence.

I spotted Lily Mai in the front row, dressed in a long flowing yellow summer dress. It was a pleasure watching her move in rhythmic sink with the group. At the head of the class was an elderly, small, spry Chinese man whose incredibly soft and effortless movement seemed to somehow command and lead the others.

I continued to watch the almost hypnotic performance for another 15 minutes until all at once it just ended. No words were spoken, and no direction was given. Everyone quietly stopped and began collecting water bottles, and discarded light jackets and bags with only a little light whispered conversation. The peacefulness of it all was startling to me.

Lily Mai approached. The elderly leader spoke a few words, and then walked directly my way. I didn't realize that she had even noticed me. She placed her hand on my arm, and it radiated with a warm energy that quickly traveled throughout my whole body. I couldn't help thinking, *"what the hell is this Tai Chi stuff?"* And before I could go any further with that thought, her sensuous gaze stopped all thoughts of anything else.

She took my hand and said, "Thank you so much for coming to meet me, Jack. I have been thinking about all that has been going on and knew that we needed to talk."

"I am glad you called," I answered as my thoughts returned to the grave business at hand. We walked through the wide square into the interior walking street lined with a double-tiered collection of Chinese businesses. We walked past numerous gift shops, restaurants and florists with shopkeepers in the process of placing their wares on display outside of their stores.

The Pavilion was already seeing some foot traffic on this sunny warm Friday morning. Lily stopped a few times to speak mostly in Chinese to shopkeepers and some passersby. *"Where is Teresa Marek when you need her?"* I thought to myself. At the end of the pavilion, we walked up a metal stairway to the last storefront on the upper level. It was a small restaurant named Ling Po BBQ.

From the outside, it didn't look open. "Are you sure they are ready for business?" I asked. "It's only 9:15."

"They will be open for me," she answered with a quiet confidence. "You see, Jack, I own this place and several others that we just walked past. They are a very minor part of my overall business in Chinatown. I make no profit here. This whole Pavilion nearly went under because of COVID. So, I and a few other prominent business leaders in this area decided to do what we could to help small Asian businesses survive. We feel that it is crucial for the neighborhood to maintain its identity and to keep these families here."

She walked up to the entrance to the Ling Po BBQ and waited for me to open the door for her. It was evident that she was used to being treated like a lady and with respect.

When we walked in, we were greeted by a middle-aged Chinese woman, dressed simply in a short-sleeved pullover light blue shirt and blue jeans. She greeted Lily in Chinese and then greeted me in English. Lily chose a table to the right and in the front of this small funky space decorated with colorful murals of unfamiliar designs and symbols. I didn't know what they were, but I liked them.

The woman brought out a pot of tea and three small cups. When I looked quizzically at Lily, she said, "I invited my Tai Chi teacher, Mr. Lui, to join us. I hope you don't mind."

I nodded and responded that was fine, even though I wondered when I would be able to actually talk seriously to her. But it was Chinatown, and I needed to be patient. A quality that didn't always come naturally to me.

Then I heard the light jingle of bells as the door opened and the spry Tai Chi teacher fairly glided into the room. Lily rose to greet him, and I instinctively did the same. The teacher motioned for us to sit down, and we followed his direction.

" Mr. Hoc Hoi Lui, this is Detective Jack Fallon." Lily said. I held out my hand and said it was a pleasure to meet him. He accepted my hand with a gentle touch. I usually wasn't a big fan of a limp handshake but it seemed fitting for Mr. Lui, who exuded calmness and serenity.

He and Lily spoke entirely in English, which I felt was in deference to me, and I appreciated it. When there was a pause in their conversation, I took the opportunity to ask some questions. I had to try to get something out of this situation.

"Mr. Lui, may I ask you a question?" I began.

The teacher turned his eyes to me and answered, "Of course, detective. How may I assist you?"

I continued. "I couldn't help but notice that several of your students were wearing shirts with the Yin Yang symbol. Does that have some special connection to your discipline?"

Mr. Lui smiled. "Oh, you have some knowledge of the meaning of the Yin and Yang?" He asked.

"Just a little." I responded. "But I am trying to learn more." I then explained in brief detail the N. Astor Street dinner party and the disappearance of the priceless Egg of Chaos.

Mr. Lui didn't say anything for what seemed like a long time, but it must have been only a couple of seconds. He appeared to be a very deliberative man.

The Tai Chi philosophy is very much based on the teachings of Lao Tze, the founder of Taoism, an ancient and respected Chinese belief in balancing nature's opposite forces acting in harmony. The water and the stone. The fire and the ice. The male and the female. It is believed that the universe emerged from the Egg of Chaos. It is a potent symbol."

"As to your problem, the mystery from the events of the dinner party at N. Astor Street, you will find all of your answers there. You must go back to the beginning. As Lao Tze teaches, a journey of a thousand miles begins with a single step."

With that, the food began arriving at the table, being served by the woman who greeted us named Ping and her teenage daughter Nico. First, they served us skewered pork, beef and chicken, and assorted vegetables, including garlic. Mushrooms were served on a long platter in individual shredded pieces with some type of oil with an unusual combination of spices. It was all accompanied by a large serving bowl of steamed jasmine rice.

It was an absolute feast. We all sampled at least one of everything before resuming our conversation. I commented that Mr. Lui had an amazing appetite and ate some of everything. I asked him about it and whether Tai Chi philosophy had any thoughts about eating meat.

Mr. Lui didn't hesitate this time. He said that he believed in taking advantage of all of the bounties God has provided to us but that we should use everything in moderation. Again, balance was the key. He went on to add that Tai Chi was very good for the digestive system and that he was thankful to have a robust appetite.

We finished our meal and enjoyed more pleasant conversation. Mr. Lui thanked Lily and said his goodbyes to our hosts and me. He then glided out the door and was gone. I felt like I had just met an extraordinary man.

Lily reached across the cleared table and placed her hand on top of mine, sending more electricity shooting through me. She whispered, "Let us go to a more private place where we can be by ourselves to talk. It is very near, and we can walk."

As we started our leisurely stroll to her apartment on S. Wentworth Ave., I asked her about the absence of the bodyguards that had been present at her nightclub and had helped protect her during the shooting. She smiled, and I melted. "You see this place," she responded, slowly waving her arm in a wide 180° movement. "I have always felt like it protects me. The people in this entire place are part of me. Of course, I realize the realities of this world. So, at times, I use security. Mostly I use it at my clubs and at night. I take precautions, but I do not want to walk my streets with armed guards or drive around in armored cars. What kind of life is that?"

I nodded and said that I understood. Danger and threats were not unfamiliar to me. We all take some risks and pay some price for our freedom and for allowing ourselves some peace of mind.

Lily's smile became even broader and brighter, and I was losing my concentration. "Do you have any idea who tried to kill you Sunday night at your club?" I asked.

She looked up at me with her dark deep brown eyes. "I really like you, Jack. You are very wise for a......." and she hesitated for a moment, "young detective."

We had only walked a couple of blocks on South Wentworth, crossing the intersection at Cermak Road along the west side of the bustling commercial street, just past the Chinatown Gate, when she stopped. "Here we are." she said. There was an entrance in between a martial arts studio and a gift shop featuring souvenirs and some type of clothing style that was a mystery to me.

After a few seconds, I again realized that she was waiting for me to open the door. When I did, she led me up a long flight of stairs to her second-floor apartment. She slid the key into the lock and turned it again, waiting for me to open the door.

I followed her into the surprisingly large apartment beautifully furnished with high ceilings and tall bay windows looking out over the street. She stopped in the middle of the front room and moved so close to me; I was having a hard time resisting the urge to put my arms around her.

"Are you going to answer my question? "I managed to ask.

"What question was that again?" She whispered so close to my face that I felt her warm breath in my mouth. It was too late. By then, I couldn't remember what the question was either. My arm slipped around her slender waist, and my left hand moved down to caress her perfectly rounded firm behind. She rose up, and I moved my head down to feel her lips performing an erotic dance with mine, and then her tongue slipped sweetly into my mouth, and we engaged in a long wet sensuous kiss.

She had brought me right to the edge and then gently pulled away just a little. "I will answer all of your questions after we get to know each other more intimately. Be patient with me, Jack. Patience is something we value highly. I wish to change out of these clothes and put on something more attractive for you." At that moment, I was thinking that I couldn't imagine being more attracted to her than I already was. She moved toward an open door that looked like it led into a bedroom. "I will be with you in just a moment. Please sit down and make yourself at home." I looked around and noticed a sofa covered in robin egg blue cloth. It crossed my mind that considering how aroused I was, it might be difficult to even sit down without taking my pants off. *"Patience Jack. Patience."*

Lily walked to the entrance of her bedroom and looked back at me. "Thank you for being so patient and understanding, Jack Fallon. It means a lot to me."

I just smiled and nodded, still wondering how to deal with my immediate predicament, when she stepped into her room and closed the door behind her.

In an instant, it was Bam! An enormous explosion blew the door off its hinges and threw me up off the floor and across the room, slamming me into the light blue couch.

Then, everything went dark.

Chapter 15

I don't know how long I was knocked out. When my eyes opened and focused, two EMTs were peering down at me with grim looks on their faces which was alarming. I blurted out her name. "Lily! You have to get Lily!" The closest EMT put her hand on my shoulder and calmly told me to sit back down as I tried to get up from the blue couch where I must have landed.

The room was still filled with smoke and fine particles of dust and debris. Two firefighters were entering Lily's bedroom through the now doorless opening. The EMT kept her hand on me and said that they needed to check me out for any injuries or signs of a concussion. "That's our job," she said. "Let the firefighters do theirs."

The EMTs spent the next 10 minutes looking me over and checking my vital signs and cognitive function. More firefighters arrived, and the two that had entered the bedroom emerged and looked at us, shaking their heads. It was finally setting in to me just how bad the blast had been. I knew Lily was gone and I felt physically and emotionally crushed before a wave of tremendous anger took over.

I bolted up from the sofa and tried to make it to Lily's room. Several of the firefighters started coming out and blocked me. I was still enraged but managed to get a hold of myself. I told them who I was and said that I was on the job. They were respectful but very firm in their response. One of them who seemed to be in charge stepped forward and made it clear. "Then, detective, you know that this is an active crime scene, and you need to get out of here and get yourself checked out at the hospital."

He was right, of course. I backed away, and the EMTs walked me out of the apartment and down the stairs out onto S. Wentworth Ave., which by then was teaming with onlookers. The sidewalk and pavement under Lily's bedroom were littered with shards of glass and brick that had been blown out by the blast.

The police cars started arriving en masse, including a couple of detectives named Bill Kroger and Dan Moncton, who approached me and introduced themselves. I gave them a complete statement as the EMTs stood by patiently. As the detectives were finishing up, the EMTs walked up and said that I needed to go with them in the ambulance.

I resisted and told everyone that I felt fine, which was completely accurate except for the ringing in my ears, the throbbing in my head, and the fact that my whole body felt like it had been pounded with a meat tenderizer. But, the EMTs were persistent, and I looked to the detectives for support, but they shrugged as if to say, *"Detective, you know the drill."*

So, I decided that a compromise was in order. I agreed to go to Northwestern Memorial emergency room, but I wanted to drive myself. The EMTs didn't like the idea, but this time I got a little help from the detectives. They promised that they would make sure that I got to Memorial, so the EMTs agreed and returned to their ambulance. While they got into their vehicle, a car from the Medical Examiner's Office pulled up, and a doctor got out carrying a medical evidence kit. Again, the reality kicked in. Lily was gone, and I wanted the perpetrators to pay. They were going to pay.

The detectives took me to my car and told me they would trust me to get to the hospital and then laughed, saying they would be calling Northwestern Memorial in 20 minutes. "You know, trust but verify."

I kept my promise and admitted myself to the Northwestern Memorial emergency room. After Dr. Fabian gave me a thorough examination, he determined that I had symptoms of a mild concussion but otherwise was unscathed, which he determined to be some sort of miracle. He gave me some extra strength Tylenol and a prescription for painkillers that I had no intention of using.

He recommended that I rest at home and not engage in any strenuous activity. I thanked him and promised to do my best. Another white lie. I was racking up the Hail Marys and Our Fathers. "Bless me, father, for I have sinned." I said out loud, chuckling and thinking if only that was the extent of it.

Once at home, I checked in with Lieutenant Whitehead and related what had gone down in Chinatown. I told him that I would rest at home for the rest of the day following the doctor's orders and that I would be good to go in the morning. Oops, there goes another one. My plan was already in motion, and I wasn't going to miss out on catching the bastards that had just murdered Lily and the others.

Morgan Latner and Henrique Sanchez had kept Agents Marek and Chan busy and passed on the information about the N. Astor Street townhouse, and Zilene had done her thing with Li Zen. The trap had been set. Now it was just a matter of which rats we would catch.

I hesitated to call Elaina because of it being her friend Chico's funeral day, but it seemed likely that the funeral mass was over by then. She answered right away and began speaking so quickly that it was challenging to keep up with her. It was clear that she had been informed about the explosion. As soon as she paused to breathe, I managed to convince her that I was fine and that we both needed to get our focus back to solving our case. She agreed, and her voice returned to her normal measured cadence. I let her know that our plan had been implemented and that we would coordinate the final game plan in the morning.

When I asked her how she was doing after the funeral, she sighed and replied that she was good. She was better now. "The funeral mass and ceremony afterward were very beautiful and emotional; she said, "I guess we both had pretty rough mornings. didn't we amigo?" she added.

"Yes, we did, partner, "I responded. "But tomorrow will be a better day." Looking out my living room windows, I could clearly see a big bright moon in the eastern sky. I knew that it would be full the next day, along with our challenge.

Saturday morning didn't come soon enough. I took some more Tylenol, but the soreness throughout my body and the headache made it difficult to sleep. Finally, I did doze off and was able to get a few hours in. When I awoke, I was relieved that the ringing in my ears had disappeared, and the headache was now barely noticeable. My body aches would take a while longer. I guess two out of three wasn't bad.

The hot shower felt fantastic, and after a long soak, I topped it off with a heavy blast of cold water. Breakfast was short and sweet—just a big bowl of Frosted Flakes and coffee. Even though I have air conditioning, the air in my apartment still felt a little warm and muggy. It was going to be a hot sticky summer day in Chicago.

Thinking about our plan most of the night, I kept coming back to a significant problem. The townhouse on N. Astor Street would be dark. We would make sure that the power would be off after 7:00 PM. I didn't think anyone who decided to go in there looking for hidden cameras, would likely turn on the lights anyway, but I wanted to make sure. The problem was that up in the library where the Consulate General was murdered would be one of the hotspots that the murderer would look for the cameras.

Consequently, I felt that Elaina and I needed to be up there lying in wait without being seen. But my problem was how do we do that? There were no closets in that room. I didn't have a clue, but I kept picturing the room and the whole house, the classic architecture and eclectic, almost gaudy decor and furniture. Then it hit me. Replaying detective movies in my mind, I kept seeing a type of movable partition from films made in the 1930s and 40s. Sometimes they were placed in the corner of the room as decoration. I couldn't remember what they were called, and I sure as hell didn't know where I could get one.

My phone call to Elaina was picked up on the third ring. And, after I explained my idea to her, she responded immediately. "Oh, you mean room dividers that fold up. They are also referred to as privacy screens." she said.

"Yes, that's it exactly!" I exclaimed. "We need to get one that is dark in color, black or dark brown and put it in the corner of the library, away from the door and the desk."

Elaina liked the plan and said it should be at least 6 1/2 feet high and go all the way down to the floor. She thought a three or four-panel privacy screen would fit pretty well into the corner of the spacious library room. We planned to meet at the Lowe's on N. Ashland Ave. in 45 minutes. In the meantime, I would let Lieutenant Whitehead know of our plan and ask him to alert the police patrol that would remain there until dark that we would be bringing the divider into the townhouse through the back of the house later that afternoon.

I also contacted Morgan Latner to make sure that he and Henrique would keep the FBI agents busy trying to find the stolen Chinese artifact. "Take them anywhere except the Chinese Consulate or N. Astor Street." I said.

Zilene was also contacted and asked to interview importer Francine Vito, and banker Harriet Bingham to reinforce that we were focusing on finding the Egg of Chaos.

I spent the next half an hour watching the Cubs play the Pirates at beautiful Wrigley Field, and icing various parts of my body. *"Somebody is going to invent a full-body ice pack one of these days."* I thought.

When it came time to meet Elaina, I put on some blue jeans, a plain white T-shirt, sneakers and a Cubs hat and hit the road in my Camaro. In less than 15 minutes, I pulled into the busy Lowe's parking lot on N. Ashland Avenue. Almost immediately after I pulled into a spot, Elaina found one a few places down from me in her Jeep Cherokee.

She was also dressed casually in jeans, a black short-sleeved shirt, and a White Sox hat. She had her hair tied up and donned sunglasses. We weren't exactly in disguise, but I thought it was a good idea to look less like detectives and more like delivery guys.

Once inside the busy Saturday afternoon crowd at Lowe's, we wound our way through the store and eventually found a display of privacy screens. After looking at several that were either too small or too light in color, we found one that fit the bill. It was a black four-panel mesh weave that was 6 1/2 feet tall. It went almost entirely down to the floor, and the weave was flexible enough that we would be able to make some very narrow slits at the right height for each of us so we would be able to see out into most of the library.

We got a hold of a salesperson who went somewhere and came back with one of the screens in a long rectangular cardboard box transported on a cart. We brought it to the checkout counter, and I put it on my card. Just another expense to voucher later.

The salesman rolled it out for us, and we walked him to Elaina's Jeep. She put down the backseat, and we were able to position the screen into her car. It wasn't too heavy, so either one of us could handle it easily. We decided to meet a couple of blocks away from the townhouse where I would Park, and we would both go in the Jeep to the alley in the back as inconspicuously as possible into the townhouse.

When we arrived at the back gate, a couple of officers were there, and they waved us to a spot in front of the townhouse garage. They were obviously expecting us. Thank you, Lieut. Whitehead.

We went through the back gate and then through the back door into the house. It seemed kind of creepy knowing what had occurred there only a week before and not knowing exactly what would happen there that night. The house was hot and humid, reflecting the weather outside, and we were sweating while walking the panels up the winding staircase to the second-floor library.

Inside the library, it was good to see plenty of room in the spacious study for the privacy screen to be placed in the corner immediately to the right of the doorway. The room itself was dark even though outside, it was sunny and clear. The panels, once set up, blended perfectly into the room, which is dominated by dark brown-black and mahogany hues.

Elaina and I were both Boy Scout prepared with pocket knives, and standing behind the screens; we were able to make subtle slits at eye level in two panels apiece. The bottom was just about an inch above the floor, but there wasn't anything we could do about that. We would have to wear black shoes.

We checked out the whole house before we left. Nothing had seemingly been disturbed since the previous Saturday night. I made sure that the front and back doors to the house were locked, since I knew that the Chinese Consulate had keys. But I wanted the doors leading to the fire escape on the second and third floors to be left open. With those things taken care of, we exited the way we came in.

Elaina dropped me off at my car, and we planned to meet that evening at 8:45 in the alley. I figured we would park on the street while the police presence was still visible. No one that we expected to show up would know our vehicles, and besides, they weren't likely to come around until after 9 PM, when the crime scene was to be released from police custody and after sunset.

I wanted to make sure that Elaina was okay with my plan before going home. We would be going into that house by ourselves with backup blocks away. We knew it could get dicey, and as I expected, my partner didn't flinch. "Of course, I am!" she responded, seeming a little insulted by my even asking.

"Great!" I responded. "Just what I expected, but I needed to ask. There's no one else I would rather have with me on this."

"All right, partner," she said. "I'll forgive you this time." We both laughed and went our ways. My ride home up Lakeshore Drive wasn't as pleasurable as usual, even though I always enjoyed looking out onto the lake and seeing the parks and beaches full of people actively having fun and taking advantage of some of the best Chicago has to offer. I was still tired and sore and preoccupied with the task at hand.

Back at home, I fixed a roast beef and cheddar sandwich with horseradish mustard on a 8" Gonnella French roll, and washed it down with a glass of milk. My couch was calling me, and I set the alarm on my phone for 7:30 before falling into a much-needed sound sleep.

My phone alarm did its job, and I woke up still feeling a bit stiff from the blast in Chinatown but refreshed and immediately alert. It was game time, and I was anxious to get it on. I dressed in a black short-sleeved crewneck T-shirt, a black cotton jacket, black slacks, and black Rockport walking shoes with black socks. I had my star and Beretta on my right hip, well hidden by the coat.

Getting into my black-on-black Chevy Camaro made me feel like some kind of secret agent man. I had to laugh. I was psyched. *Man, I love this job,* I thought. *This is really what I live for.*

On the drive to the Gold Coast neighborhood, I called Lieut. Whitehead and found out that everything was in place for my plan. I told him that Elaina and I would put our phones on total silence as soon as we met up a couple of blocks away from the townhouse. We would be using texts to communicate between ourselves once we got inside, no later than 9 PM. He said he would pull the police patrol off the townhouse right at nine, with instructions for a couple of cars to stay in the neighborhood but no closer than three blocks away. He also said, "Good luck Jack. You two take care of yourselves. I don't want any more casualties, and that's an order."

At the Gold Coast, I decided to take a parking spot on Goethe Street between North Astor and State Street. There were a couple of open spaces left, and within a minute, Elaina pulled her Jeep Cherokee into one of them.

We exited our vehicles and gave each other a high five. "Ready to go, partner?" I asked with a smile.

"I was born ready!" she replied seriously.

We silenced our phones and were ready for action. She was decked out in all black, and had her game face on. Great intensity. I loved it.

The wide alley that ran between North Astor Street and State Street was quiet and deserted. It was starting to get dark, and the alley was dimly lit. The brightest source of light was the full moon hanging in the eastern sky over Lake Michigan, which was only a couple of blocks away.

We walked north up the alley without saying a thing or seeing a soul. As we approached the back of the townhouse, I looked at the dumpster nearby and remembered the kick to the head I had received from one of those little ninja assholes. I felt a surge of adrenaline, and my mood got darker.

At the back gate, we quietly greeted the two officers standing guard. They hadn't seen or heard anything all night. The coast seemed to be clear for now. We told them that we were going up the fire escape to enter the library on the second floor. As soon we were in, I asked them to wait a couple of minutes before clearing out. It was almost nine anyway and almost entirely dark.

We entered the library through the door next to the fire escape second-floor landing. We both had small flashlights but didn't use them. The moonlight provided enough illumination, and we knew the room's layout well enough to find our way.

I entered the space behind the black meshed room divider, and Elaina followed. She was closest to the door leading into the room from the hallway, and adjusted the outside panel to ensure that she couldn't be seen by anyone entering.

We waited without saying a word, and I have to admit the suspense was making me a little edgy. The occasional sound of a car door closing or a siren off in the distance was a little unsettling.

I decided to send Elaina a text just to break the monotony. "How are your feet holding up?" I asked in text. "I'm good," she responded. "And you?" "I'm fine; my Rockports are comfortable. Just getting a little antsy."

"Me too." She messaged. "I guess neither one of us is good with waiting."

"Yeah," I responded. "Patience may be a virtue, but it's not one of mine…"

And then, we heard what sounded like the front door on the first floor being unlocked and then opened. There were footsteps and whispering from several voices. The chatter was low but definitely not English. I had a pretty good idea what language it was, though.

Elaina looked over to me and smiled that kind of smile that was more of a warning than a warm greeting. I gave her the thumbs up and knew we were ready. Noises that sounded like things were being moved around downstairs, suggesting that they were looking for something. Hidden cameras came to mind. Footsteps could be heard on the staircase and then in the hallway.

The library door was opened slowly and then in walked Deputy Consulate Generals Li Qjang Yong and Fong Wu accompanied by Security Chief Yi Peng and one of the little ninja bastards. The ninja carried a small device with a wand-like attachment. He started using the wand to try to detect hidden cameras, I surmised.

The consulate officials spoke in Chinese and walked over to the large desk, and the scary-looking Security Chief motioned for Deputy Consulate General Li Yong to sit down, which he did.

151

What the hell is going on? I wondered. Are they all together in this, or are the two men setting up Fong Wu and looking to finish her off after missing the attempt outside the consulate? The ninja kept probing different areas of the room with his wand and eventually stood right in front of us and the room divider. I felt certain that he would move it, but he just waved his little stick and turned to say something in Chinese. I didn't have any idea what he said, but whatever it was, it seemed to spur Yi Peng into action. He pulled a light rope out of his coat pocket and wrapped it around the sitting Deputy General Yong. He was swift. In a matter of seconds, Deputy Yong was pinned to the chair, and Lurch was pushing up the sleeve of his jacket and starting to unbutton his white shirt sleeve and rolling it up, exposing his arm.

Fong Wu pulled out a small vial of liquid and a syringe. *"Wow!"* I thought. She really had me fooled. Li Yong was the odd man out. We had to make our move. I looked at Elaina as I drew my gun and made a motion like a push toward the divider. She got it immediately and drew her pistol. I counted 1,2,3 with my fingers, and on three, we both forcefully threw the partition forward and down.

The force of the divider knocked the ninja down and startled the others. We charged over the black panels trampling the ninja. Lurch was super quick and drew his gun and fired a shot that whistled right between my partner and me. My first shot caught him in the neck, and he groaned and raised his left hand to try to stop the gushing blood that was pouring out. Incredibly, he didn't drop the gun in his right hand. As he raised his arm, my second shot hit him in the chest near his right shoulder, causing him to spin, drop the gun, and fall behind the desk.

Deputy General Yong looked terrified but didn't utter a word. I thought he was probably going into shock, but there was no time for that now. Elaina was engaged in a struggle over the syringe with Fong Wu, and I knew how that would turn out. So, I focused on the little jagoff who had sprung to his feet right next to me. He had a

152

pistol in his belt but didn't go for it. I guess he wanted to take me on mano a mano. That suited me just fine.

His distance from me was perfect for him to land a direct frontal kick, so anticipating that, I sidestepped his move just in time and grabbed his right leg with both hands, and lifted it, giving me a clear opening for a kick of my own. I made a direct hit to his groin, and he howled. While still holding his right leg, I used my right foot to crash down hard on his left knee cap, and he yelled out again and crumpled to the floor.

Looking back at Elaina, I saw her take Fong Wu down with a trip move, but the Chinese woman was strong and nimble, and didn't let go of the syringe.

Just then, I heard footsteps out on the fire escape. In a flash, the door flung open, and ninja number two bolted into the room carrying one of those electronic detectors. He threw it at me and charged right behind it. I managed to duck the machine which flew over my head. He began reaching for his pistol but got too close to me, and I kicked it out of his hand. He didn't hesitate and tried a straight kick which I again was able to sidestep, but he immediately followed up with a spinning backhand punch using his left hand. But I saw this one coming too. I ducked and came up and grabbed his right arm and slammed it over my right knee. He screamed in pain, and I could see that it was a clean break. His right arm hung limp at his side, and I grabbed his left arm, placed a handcuff on it, dragged him over to the other ninja who was writhing in pain on the floor, forced him down next to him, and placed the other cuff on the first ninja's right wrist.

By this time, Elaina was finishing cuffing Fong Wu's hands behind her back. Then I heard a noise coming from the first floor. I looked at Elaina, and she said, "Go, Jack!" I've got this.

I ran to the stairs and charged down them. At the bottom, it was dark, and I needed to move gingerly, since I wasn't as familiar with the layout down there as I was in the library. I moved into the large dining room, where I saw one turned-over chair and someone attempting to climb onto one of the other chairs. I grabbed the man at the knees and slammed him face down onto the dining room table with a thud and a groan.

I flipped the guy over and couldn't believe my eyes. It was fucking Professor Nils Borland.

"What in the hell are you doing here?" I demanded in disbelief. He shook his head but didn't say anything. I got him seated in a chair at the table and said, thinking out loud. "This is fucking unbelievable!" *What is this nerdy art professor doing mixed up with some kind of international drug deal?* It was beyond me, and he wasn't talking.

Elaina must have called in the reinforcements, because officers began pouring into the townhouse. I told them to cuff Prof. Borland and have him charged with trespassing and tampering with evidence for now.

Next, EMTs came rushing in, and I sent them upstairs. Other officers were directed to clear the entire place and create a new crime scene.

As Borland was being led out, he kept looking back. I thought he was looking at me at first, but his eyes were gazing above me toward the ceiling, or was it something else. I looked up, and the light from the moon shone right onto the impressive five-layered crystal chandelier. And then —it hit me. I jumped up onto a chair and then the table. I bent down, peered into the large first layer of the chandelier, and there it was. I reached into it, and nestled in among the colored crystals, was the priceless jade and gold Egg of Chaos. "Holy shit!!" I roared and jumped down to the floor.

"Elaina!" I yelled at the top of my lungs. "We've got it! We found the god damn Egg of Chaos!"

Chapter 16

I flew up the stairs two at a time and burst into the library where EMTs were attending to one large Chinese security chief and two tiny Chinese assassins. They were all in pretty bad shape, but I can't say that I felt their pain. Elaina had Deputy Consulate General Fong Wu handcuffed and sitting on the couch. She had untied Deputy General Li Qjang Yong, and he was still sitting in the executive chair behind the desk and was still looking shellshocked.

Elaina jumped up from the couch and gave me a hard high-five. She was nearly as excited as I was about recovering the Egg. I couldn't wait to deliver the news to Curator Belinda Carlisle. After all, I had boldly promised her that I would get it back for the Art Institute.

Soon Curator Carlisle answered the phone call, and within seconds, her somber mood changed to jubilation. I asked her what she wanted me to do with it, and she said that she would be right there to pick it up and get it back to the Art Institute immediately. We usually would keep something like that as evidence, but since it never left the premises, it wasn't actually stolen, and she was adamant that the museum did not want any publicity about the incident and had no interest in pressing any charges.

Elaina and I huddled and decided to interrogate the two deputy counsel generals right there. They both had diplomatic immunity, and we had a short window of opportunity to question them before the politicians got involved and we lost them. I decided to take Fong Wu to another room on the second floor and leave Li Qjang to my partner.

Lurch was in no shape to talk with a bullet in his neck and probably wouldn't have, no matter his condition. The other two were in a great deal of pain and were speaking only in Chinese.

They would be taken to the hospital under arrest and interrogated later.

Before getting started with Fong Wu, I called Morgan Latner and got him up to speed and told him that he could release agents Marek and Chan from whatever wild goose chase he had them on and that I would give him the whole story in the morning. There was no need to tell the agents much yet. There was still the issue of the rouge special agent supervisor to deal with.

I also called Zilene Baker and was happy to learn that she was at the station where they were taking Prof. Nils Borland. After giving her the basics of what had gone down on N. Astor Street, I asked her to see what she could get out of the professor and that if he balked, she could try telling him that we found the ancient artwork and we had him on a hidden camera placing it in the chandelier. It was BS and only a hunch, but I figured it was worth a try.

I walked Deputy Consulate General Fong Wu into a sitting room down the hall from the library and sat her down in an armchair while I stood over her, looking and sounding as menacing as I could. I made some baseless threats about spending the rest of her life in a hard-core American prison, and her tough, confident façade melted away. It turned out that she was petrified of going to jail.

She sang like a beautiful Asian songbird. She gave up everybody and laid out the whole scheme. I was surprised and impressed that their plan to bring vast quantities of heroin into the United States was closer to succeeding than we thought.

Her partners in China had been developing poppy fields in southern China for several years. With the help of some major exporters from Shanghai like Li Zen, they were ready to ship tons of the stuff in containers placed among thousands of legitimate products being shipped out of Shanghai Port.

The last steps were getting large-scale importers like Maxi-Mart to accept the shipments and put them into a distribution chain with financing provided by bankers like Harriet Bingham. The local sellers would be young Chinese Street gangs from Chinatown and Argyle Street, in partnership with some of the smaller Latino gangs that felt left out by the Latin Kings and the Mexican cartels.

I couldn't help thinking about what Detective José Santos had said about causing a gang war bloodbath. I also couldn't help thinking that he was right. There was no way the Mexican cartels or the Latin Kings etc. would have put up with it. No way!

Fong Wu gave up all the other players, including Yi Peng, the security chief. Banker, Harriet Bingham, importer Francine Vito, Li Zen, and Henry long were also thrown under the bus. They were all part of the conspiracy to import and sell the heroin and to murder anyone that got in their way. Grace Tobin, Harry Sachman, Lily Mai Tong, and Dominic Blasi; all were offered a chance to participate, and when they refused, they had to go. Only Dominic Blasi managed to survive the assassination attempts.

The Chinese Consulate officials were also either on board with the plan or a problem to be eliminated. Fong said she knew the Consulate Gen. Zhao Chen would never have gone along and was never told about it. He was simply murdered by Security Chief Yi Peng. She had hoped that her counterpart, Deputy Consulate Gen. Li Qjang, would join them, but when it became clear that he would not, they decided to get rid of him the same way they disposed of FBI Agent Kira Vu Sing. They were tipped off about her by Supervising Special Agent William Manion, who was offered an enormous amount of money for his information and protection. The apparent attempt on her life in front of the consulate was a ruse to deflect any suspicion from her.

Fong Wu claimed to know nothing about the missing Egg of Chaos, and I believed her. She didn't know anything about art. That was a passion of Consulate General Zhao Chen. Arranging for the artwork to be brought to the dinner party was completely his idea, and she had reluctantly gone along with it.

The whole townhouse was now filling up with officers and crime scene investigators. I told a couple of uniformed officers to take Fong Wu under arrest and keep her under wraps until further notice. We wouldn't be able to hold her very long, but I was hoping for just long enough to round up the rest of the gang before they found out about this.

I went to the library where Elaina was finishing up with Li Qjang Yong. She pulled me aside and said, "Jack, he's still scared to death. I don't think he had anything to do with the heroin deal or the murders."

"You're right." I responded. "Fong Wu confirmed it. She gave up everybody and said Li Qjang wasn't involved and was going to be given a hotshot because of it. I think we can let him go."

We got out of the way of the CSI guys and went outside to wait for the detectives that would be there to take our pistols and interview us. I took the Egg of Chaos with me.

Even after dark, the night seemed to be getting warmer. There was a stiff breeze from the south bringing in hot, humid air. I took my jacket off and hung it over the wrought iron fence. The night sky was clear, and the bright full moon dominated.

While we were waiting, a black sedan stopped in the street right in front of us. The driver's door swung open, and a short slight figure darted out and rushed toward us. It was Curator Belinda Chin Carlisle. She approached us, practically hyperventilating. She could hardly speak. She didn't need to. I held out the precious artwork to her holding it in both hands. She opened the lid from a solid mahogany box lined with thick felt padding. I gently placed the Egg of Chaos inside, and she shut the lid carefully and latched it.

"I can't tell you how much this means to me, the museum, and the whole art world. And I can't thank you enough." She hugged us both awkwardly since she was gripping the mahogany box like a fullback running through the line of scrimmage. As she got into her car and drove off, Elaina and I both had broad smiles on our faces.

Soon the detectives arrived, and we spent the next hour giving statements and turning over our guns. During that time, I kept Lieut. Whitehead informed, and he told me to let the team know that we had done a great job and to report to him the following day at 10.

When the dust cleared and the detectives were gone, we were done for the night. Elaine and I walked to our cars on Goethe Street without saying much of anything. Her vehicle was nearest, and we stopped in front of it on the sidewalk. We gave each other another high five. "I don't know about you, but I'm exhausted." I said.

"Definitely!" she answered. "It's been one hell of a week. See you, tomorrow compadre."

"Okay, partner. See you in the morning." I said while walking to my Camaro, two cars away.

When I got in, I laid my jacket on the passenger seat. My phone was in the inside pocket, and I took it out and took the mute setting off. At that moment the phone rang and showed an unknown number. Something told me to answer it. The voice, on the other end, was familiar and sent a surge of excitement through my body. It was Emma Merlin. In an instant, I was alert and energized.

"Hi, Jack Fallon. I was sorry you couldn't make the after-party last Saturday. How did your case turn out?" She asked.

I had to laugh. "Well, it's been crazy all week, but we just wrapped it up."

"So, you're not busy?"

I am totally not busy," I responded enthusiastically.

"Great!" She said. "Where would you like to meet?"

"I know just the place for a night like this. Can you meet me at Montrose Beach in about 15 minutes? I'm headed right there."

"Sure can," she answered. "See you there."

I climbed into my car, turned on the engine and some tunes, put the top down and thought, "How cool is that!"

The drive to Uptown and Montrose Beach was like flying on air. The warm breeze rushed in from the open windows and open air, and the pounding beat of the music was a fantastic rush. I called Lieut. Whitehead and asked him for a favor. Under the circumstances, he was in a generous mood, so he readily agreed to contact the Uptown District and make sure that the night patrol was aware that I would be down at the beach with company and would ensure us some privacy.

At the beach parking lot, I was happy to see no other cars. It was empty except for a lone bicycle way off to the far end of the lot. I placed my Star in the glove compartment with my wallet, put the windows most of the way up, and closed the roof.

There was only some indirect light from the city and the moon; illuminating the beach. I spotted a small female figure sitting near the water. When I got closer, I recognized the strawberry blonde hair and curvy shape of Emma Merlin. I sat down next to her, and she reached over and placed her hand on my thigh and just said, "Hi there, Jack."

I couldn't hide my excitement. She laughed, stood up, and blithely pulled her summer dress over her head and dropped it on the sand, revealing her diminutive yet gorgeously voluptuous body. "Let's go for a swim." She said with an enticing smile.

No words came out of my mouth. I stood up and shed my clothes in an instant. We walked to the Lake directly into the shining path laid down from the sky above and began swimming. After going out about 50 yards, we stopped and embraced, enjoying the magical moonlight and each other fully for the first time.

Epilogue

Within a week, all of the suspects were picked up and charged with conspiracy to commit first-degree murder in Illinois and federal racketeering charges. Herbert Long was nabbed right away on Saturday night at one of his restaurants on Argyle Street. Harriet Bingham and Francine Vito were arrested at their offices on Monday morning, and Li Zen was apprehended a few days later at JFK airport in New York, while waiting to board a plane to Shanghai.

Fong Wu was released Sunday morning but not before giving a fully recorded statement, after being read her Miranda rights just to be safe. Yi Peng was going to be in intensive care for a while, but he and Fong Wu were covered under diplomatic immunity. I couldn't help but wonder what fate awaited them back in China. I figured that justice would be served.

The little ninja bastards did turn out to be Chinese citizens, but they were not officially employed by the Chinese Consulate, so there was no immunity for them. They were both treated at the hospital, released to police custody, and charged with the murders of Grace Tobin, Harry Sachman, and Lily Mai Tong, as well as the attempted murders of Dominic Blasi and Detective Koslowski.

There were no commendations or fanfare this time. Fortunately, no police officers had been killed. The Mayor and top state officials had no interest in any publicity on this one. That was all fine with Elaina and me. We were ready to move on. There were thousands of interesting stories in the City of Chicago, and this had been one of them. We both knew there were plenty more to come.

During that next week, a young Latino man was found dead in an alley early one morning in Pilsen. He was entangled in a red mountain bike with the chain somehow wrapped tightly around his neck. The police theorized that he had been carrying a pistol in his belt, and it discharged, blowing away most of his groin after the man hit a pothole and the bike flipped over. They described it as an unfortunate accident and warned the public of the danger of carrying loaded weapons. The Medical Examiner's Office ruled the cause of death was exsanguination, and the manner of death was accidental. Case closed.

Prof. Nils Borland admitted sneaking back into the townhouse while the smoke was still thick. He went up to the library and saw the Consulate General sitting there dead but didn't hesitate to take the artifact and run back downstairs. Passing through the dining room, he heard the firefighters coming inside and put the Egg of Chaos up into the crystal chandelier, thinking that he would be able to return for it later.

The professor wasn't charged since he never took it out of the house, and the Art Institute didn't want to pursue it. However, his obsession with the priceless artwork cost him his job with the University of Chicago. He resigned before the story got out to avoid embarrassment.

My night with Emma was magical and everything I imagined it would be. We parted ways after watching a spectacular sunrise. I still didn't have her number. But she is such a unique and free-spirited woman; that I decided to live with it. However, I did allow myself to look forward to the next time.

Printed in the USA
CPSIA information can be obtained
at www.ICGtesting.com
LVHW060339220524
780971LV00010B/151